Shadow Gifts
Rachel Lynne

SEVEN OAKS PRESS

WITH MY COMPLIMENTS

Beneath the moss-laden oaks, secrets stir with the tides ...

Contents

Thank You for Joining Me in the Shadows!

Claim Your Free Signed Bookplate

I'd love to send you a signed bookplate! Just email me at rachel@rachellynneauthor.com with your mailing address.

Discover the Treasure Hunt

Hidden within the map of Savannah are seven ghosts and a secret icon is hidden in one of the chapter images.

Find the icon in this story and keep track as each book reveals a new piece of the puzzle.

Find them all, decipher the message, and visit my website for a special reward!

Happy hunting—and may the shadows guide your way!

Stay Curious,

Rachel

I

FIRST IMPRESSIONS

I stepped off the bus, my feet hitting the pavement of the Savannah terminal with a sense of finality. The bus doors closed behind me with a hiss of air and a heavy clunk, as if sealing off the past that I couldn't remember.

Refusing to let my mind wander to dark places, I took a deep breath and entered the building. Hopping on the first bus leaving Atlanta had been impulsive, but now I needed a plan and first up was finding a place to stay, preferably a cheap one.

Cajoling a nice older woman at the service counter into doing an internet search, I was soon in possession of an address for a youth hostel that only wanted sixty bucks a night.

Only! I snorted, hitching my worn leather duffle higher on my shoulder as I left the terminal. The hospital's thousand-dollar check from a victim's advocacy group was already dwindling after one night in Atlanta, food, and a bus ticket. Sixty bucks for the hostel would barely leave me with seven hundred, and I'd need a job—fast.

I pushed the worry aside and took in my surroundings. The bus station was in a rundown, semi-industrial area, but a few blocks later, I stepped into Savannah's historic district. I could see why tourists flocked here—the change was stark and the brochure I'd grabbed at the terminal hadn't done it justice.

Weathered brick paths lined with towering live oaks draped in Spanish moss led me past stately homes, where glimpses of secret gardens peeked through wrought iron gates as the sun dipped lower.

A gust of wind rustled the trees, sending a shiver down my spine. Savannah might be coastal, but in early March, the evening air was cold enough to wish for a warmer coat.

Picking up my pace, I reached the hostel—a charming, weathered Victorian with a "Vacancy" sign in the window. After checking in and dropping my duffle onto the bed, my stomach reminded me I hadn't eaten since before the bus ride.

Following the desk clerk's directions, I soon found myself in Forsyth Park. The park's gas lamps cast a warm glow over brick paths, and the grand fountain at its center shimmered in the fading light. I paused for a moment, captivated by its beauty, but a growling stomach urged me to keep moving.

As I left the park, I noticed two women in elaborate gowns approaching on a side path. Not the first time I'd seen people in odd clothing—earlier, I'd passed a guy in an old gray uniform with a sword, and a horse-drawn carriage carrying a formally dressed couple. Dismissing them as actors, I turned to leave.

But then, a thick fog rolled in, swallowing the path in an instant. The women vanished, leaving only swirling mist behind. I scanned the area for cameras or a movie crew—nothing. Just me, the heavy fog, and...whispers. Faint at first, indistinct, like fragments of a forgotten conversation.

The whispers grew louder, like a crowd just beyond reach. My pulse quickened and a cold prickle crawled up my spine. I couldn't shake the unsettling feeling of being watched.

But no. There had to be an explanation—this was Savannah, after all. Tourists, actors, something.

The mist clung to me, icy tendrils seeping into my bones. I stood frozen for a moment, nerves jangling, before shaking my head. Get it together. *This is what happens when you skip meals.*

Rubbing my arms, I picked up the pace and hurried out of the park, putting the strange whispers and fog behind me. Time to stop messing around and find something to eat.

Savannah was a city made for walking. The neighborhoods around the park were mostly residential, but every few blocks, a small green space interrupted the streets, each one marked as something-or-other square. Fountains and monuments occupied the centers, surrounded by benches that invited people to linger. Maybe one day I would, but tonight I had a mission—cheap food.

As the homes gave way to bars and restaurants, I checked the menus hanging by the doors. Too pricey for my budget. Walking the streets felt like a step back in time and more costumed actors added to that effect. I wondered again if there was some kind of reenactment or movie shoot happening.

The hostel's brochure had mentioned Savannah's popularity with Hollywood, but so far, I hadn't stumbled on any movie sets. Maybe tomorrow I'd explore more—who knew, maybe I could even score a gig as an extra.

But my stomach had other priorities. Picking up the pace, I passed through a small park—Madison Square, the sign said—and finally spotted the Crescent Moon Tavern. Pub food might fit the budget...

I was about to cross the street when an icy sensation crept over my skin. I glanced back at the square. The giant oak trees were perfectly still, no wind in sight. So why the sudden chill?

Someone tugged on my jacket. "Excuse me, miss..."

I spun around to find a little girl in a Victorian-style dress. I grinned. "Hi, are you going to a party?"

The girl tilted her head, confusion clouding her expression. "Please, miss, can you tell me where to find Solomon's Apothecary? Mother isn't well, and someone at the boarding house told me to fetch a tincture, but I can't find the—"

"I'm sorry," I interrupted, shivering as the air grew colder. "I've only been in Savannah a few hours."

A nagging pulse next to my right eye signaled the headache that was coming. Food was a priority, but first, I needed to help this kid. I rubbed my forehead and turned to point at a nearby newsstand. "Why don't you ask for directions over there..."

But when I looked back, she was gone. Not just moved—vanished.

I checked both sides of the street and the alley, but there was no sign of her. With a shrug, I crossed the street and scanned the tavern's menu.

The daily special—a cheeseburger, fries, and a drink for fifteen dollars—was going to eat into my budget, but it couldn't be helped. Warmth returned to my body, and the throbbing in my temples had eased, but a good meal would ensure it didn't come back.

The pub's interior was rustic, with exposed brick walls and wood-beamed ceilings. A fireplace occupied one wall, surrounded by clusters of tables, while a staircase led to a balcony flanking a pool table. A long oak bar stretched along the opposite side.

I took a seat at the bar and people-watched while waiting for my food. The vibrant orange and lavender sunset had faded into darkness when a burst of laughter drew my attention to the door. A group of fifteen or twenty people entered, led by an older man who herded them into a circle near the fireplace.

I grinned. The man's white linen suit and manicured goatee made him look like he'd stepped out of an old Southern painting. Curious, I glanced at the bartender. "What's that all about?"

He smirked. "Giles's nightly haunted pub tour."

My brows lifted. "This pub is haunted?"

He shrugged. "So they say."

A server placed my food in front of me. "Need anything else?" he asked, handing the bartender a ticket.

I shook my head and spread mustard on the bun as I half-listened to the guide's storytelling. My lips curved in an indulgent smile as he spun outlandish tales of pirates, duels, and star-crossed lovers haunting the pub.

I was finishing the fries when a collective gasp from the group drew my attention back to the tour.

The guide had led the group to the second-floor balcony. The bar was packed now, and the rising noise drowned out most of what the guide said, but I managed to catch parts of the story—something about a card sharp caught cheating and a gunfight.

I was piecing together the details when movement farther along the balcony made me blink. A man hovered outside a closed door, dressed in an old-fashioned black suit and bowler hat. My eyes widened when I spotted the gun in his hand.

"Excuse me." I turned, catching the bartender's attention. "That man has a gun! Is he part of the tour?" I pointed toward the balcony.

The bartender frowned, following my gaze. "Lady, what are you talking about? Guns aren't allowed in here."

I huffed, spinning back to the balcony. "Well, someone should tell that guy because he didn't get the memo. Wait...where did he go?"

I looked back at the bartender just in time to see him roll his eyes. My lips tightened and I started to argue, but he was already moving down the bar, shaking his head.

Perplexed, I tried to make sense of what I'd seen while finishing my meal. No matter what the bartender said, I knew I'd seen a man with a gun. Was it part of the tour? I was still debating when the tour guide approached the bar.

"Thirsty group tonight, Jim. I think they're planning to stick around." The guide set an envelope on the counter. "Give Lenny my thanks for letting us include the Crescent in the tour."

Jim nodded, stashing the envelope in the cash register. "Will do, Giles. Can I get you one for the road?"

The older man smiled and slid onto the stool next to me. "A dram of whiskey would hit the spot, thank you."

I watched the guide in the mirror behind the bar. He looked younger than I'd originally thought—late fifties, maybe early sixties. From his joking tone with Jim, he seemed like a friendly sort.

Curious about the man I'd seen on the balcony, I waited until Jim stepped away. "I caught bits of your stories. Interesting." I laughed. "And the actor on the balcony was a nice touch."

He tilted his head. "Thank you." His brow furrowed slightly. "Pardon me, but did you say actor?"

"Yeah," I nodded. "The guy in the old-fashioned suit. Gotta admit, when I saw the gun, I nearly ducked under the table until I figured he was part of your tour. I even alerted the bartender, but he didn't see him."

His lips curved into a half-smile as he leaned in slightly. "Would you mind describing this actor for me?"

I narrowed my eyes. What was his game? But deciding to humor him, I replied, "Late thirties, maybe early forties? Black three-piece suit, bowler hat, handlebar mustache. Looked like a proper old-time gunslinger or gambler. Really added to your spiel."

His smile twitched. "Ah yes, my 'spiel.'" He tossed back the rest of his whiskey, then offered his hand. "Giles Westlake, proprietor of Shades of Savannah historical ghost tours."

"Lenox Grady. Nice to meet you." I shook his hand, then tilted my head. "Do you use actors for other parts of the tour? I've seen a lot of people in costume tonight. Figured they were filming a movie or something."

His brow arched, his gaze steady on mine. "Ah, yes. Our city does see its fair share of movie productions, but I'm not aware of any currently shooting here. Where did you see these actors?"

I shrugged. "Around town. I'm staying at a hostel near the big park and walked over from there."

He nodded thoughtfully. "I see. And you're sure they were in costume? Can you describe them?"

I stifled a huff. I wasn't a historian. How would I know? "I'm not sure. Some looked like they were in Civil War uniforms, and a couple of women were in long dresses with, uh, the back all puffed out." I motioned behind me, feeling a little ridiculous.

"Ah," Giles nodded, "a bustle. Popular for women in the late 1800s." He paused, watching me for a beat before clearing his throat. "My dear, I don't use actors for my tours."

"But I saw him!" I blurted, cutting him off. "He was standing on that balcony, aiming a gun at the pool table."

"And Jim didn't notice this man?" Giles's gaze remained steady, unnerving in its calmness.

I scowled. "No, but he must've ducked through one of those doors before Jim turned around..." His expression didn't change, but I rushed on, knowing I sounded defensive. "I'm telling you, he was there. Dressed like an old-timey gunslinger. Are you really going to sit there and tell me I imagined it?"

Giles leaned forward, elbows resting on the bar, hands propping up his chin as he studied me. He didn't say anything for so long that I thought I'd offended him. Just as I opened my mouth to apologize, he cleared his throat.

"Ms. Grady," he began, his voice lower, more serious, "what do you know about the spirit world?"

I blinked. The spirit world? Seriously? Was he for real? I didn't have time for this kind of talk, especially from someone who looked like he'd just stepped out of a Southern gothic novel.

"What, like ghosts and ghouls and stuff?"

He nodded slowly. "Yes. The supernatural world. Are you familiar with it?"

I let out a sharp laugh, but it held no humor. "Uh, only that it's not real." Sliding off the barstool, I grabbed my jacket.

This guy was either drunk or crazy and I was not sticking around to find out which. "I really need to get going. Nice meeting you, though."

"A moment, if you please," he called after me, his voice steady. I froze as his hand gently clasped my forearm.

"Really," I said, tugging my arm free. "It's late. Bedtime."

Giles released me with a smile, reaching into his waistcoat. "I understand. But before you go, I'd like you to have this."

He produced an ivory-colored business card, handing it to me with a slight flourish. "Feel free to call—or better yet, drop by." He gestured out the window. "My home is just down the street on Monterey Square. I work late hours, so after nine will suit."

I took the card without thinking, eyeing him warily. "Thanks, but...why should I?"

His lips twitched, and a spark of amusement danced in his eyes. "Why, to discuss your ability to see ghosts, of course."

2

SIGHT UNSEEN

I checked out of the hostel early the next morning, my dwindling finances weighing me down more than my duffle bag. With no plan and a growing sense of dread, I set off toward the park I'd passed last night, barely registering the world around me.

My stomach churned with worry as I wondered if I'd made the right decision. Should I have stayed in Atlanta? At least there, I had some support from social services.

Sighing, I walked through Forsyth Park, the sound of horse-drawn carriages and tourists only heightening my sense of isolation. As I passed the fountain, my gaze fell on a homeless man in a wheelchair, a tattered sign resting on his lap: "Vet, please help."

I swallowed hard, reminding myself that, as tough as things were, I still had options. It was time to stop feeling sorry for myself and find a way forward. Wiping away a tear, I squared my shoulders and set off down Barnard Street, scanning for help-wanted signs.

It was a tourist town—there had to be work somewhere. I stopped in at an antique store, then a few bars, but each rejection chipped away at my confidence. With every polite "sorry, we're not hiring," the knot of anxiety tightened in my chest. My determination was slipping fast, and despair was settling in.

My chest tightened, and a cold sweat broke out on my forehead. *I can't keep doing this.* The familiar panic was setting in. I forced myself to take a deep breath, clenching my fists. *You have to keep trying,* I reminded myself, even though the words felt hollow.

Fighting off the rising tide of depression, I continued down the street until I reached Chatham Square. The moss-draped oaks and neatly trimmed lawns offered a momentary respite, but even here, I couldn't escape the weight of my thoughts.

I plopped onto a bench, my body tired from walking and my mind worn down from the constant stream of rejection. The faint scent of flowers drifted through the air, carried by the breeze that stirred the Spanish moss overhead. The moss fluttered like ghostly tendrils, clinging to the ancient oaks.

I rolled my eyes. I had ghosts on the brain, and it was all that tour guide's fault!

Giles's words had rattled around in my head all night, refusing to leave me in peace. *Ghosts*. What a ridiculous idea. I didn't come to Savannah to chase ghost stories—I came here to rebuild my life, to figure out who I was. So why was I letting some old man's ramblings get under my skin?

I didn't need this. Between the old man's ghost nonsense and the nightmares, I hadn't had a wink of sleep.

I gulped, my throat tightening as I recalled the nightmare. It was always the same—a lavish party in some kind of gallery. I'd ignore the fancy-dressed people and stare at the paintings, but last night, the serene landscape had shifted, morphing into a terrifying run through a dark forest. And as usual, I'd been wearing that strange blue ballgown with the golden snake, its emerald eyes glowing...

I shivered, pushing the image away. It was just a dream, nothing more. But still, everything felt off today. Like the dream, like Savannah itself, had stirred something beneath the surface.

I rubbed my temples, trying to clear my head. I needed a distraction.

A burst of laughter pulled me from my thoughts. Across the square, a young boy was playing with an old-fashioned hoop and stick. I frowned. *Weird toy for a kid in the age of video games.* And... what was he wearing? *Breeches?*

I stared, curiosity rising despite myself. The conversation with Giles came rushing back. *Ghosts.*

Maybe I had to confront this head-on. Enough guessing. The only way to get rid of these thoughts was to prove to myself once and for all that I wasn't seeing ghosts.

I stood up, stomach churning as I crossed the square. The closer I got, the more the air seemed to thicken, a heaviness moving in. My footsteps slowed as the boy continued to play, unaware of my approach.

"Excuse me," I called. "Can I ask you something?"

He turned and looked at me, wide-eyed and silent. I took a step closer.

And then, right before my eyes, his solid little body grew hazy. My heart stuttered. He blinked, and then...he faded. Just vanished into thin air.

I froze, breath stuck in my throat and swiped at my eyes. *No way. No way!*

Panic seized my lungs. I backed away, but my feet tangled on the uneven brick path. A broken breath escaped me. Fight or flight kicked in hard—flight winning.

Without a second thought, I bolted.

My legs moved on instinct, carrying me down the narrow streets, through alleys—my heart pounding with terror. The shadows of townhomes loomed overhead, dark and suffocating, but I couldn't stop. I had to get away. From what, I didn't know—but my mind screamed *run*.

Finally, lungs burning, I stumbled out of the alley and onto Bull Street. The bustling thoroughfare was a stark contrast to the shadowy streets I'd just fled. Gasping for air, I slowed my frantic pace, leaning against the nearest building, trying to steady my racing heart.

I slid into a crouch, the warm brick at my back helping to ground me. As my breathing evened out, the familiar sights of tourists snapping photos and locals shopping brought me back to reality. *It was just a trick of the light,* I told myself. Stress and hunger, nothing more. *You need a job, not ghost stories!*

I gave myself a shake, willing the fear away. *Snap out of it.* The sharp scent of roasted coffee and vanilla wafted by, and I let it pull me out of my daze. Caffeine might help steady my nerves.

I followed the smell to a two-story brick building, its buttery yellow trim catching the sun. The Quill and Brew, the sign read. The small round tables inside were full, but a long line moved steadily toward the counter. If nothing else, maybe they were hiring.

Stepping inside, I took my place at the end of the line, scanning the café. College students with textbooks, people typing away on laptops—it felt like a normal place. A safe place.

Then the temperature dropped.

I froze, the fine hairs on the back of my neck standing on end. The throb in my head returned, sharp and sudden.

A surge of energy rippled through the café, followed by a strange flash of light. And then, I heard it—a soft melody, familiar but eerie. "Moon River."

I turned, searching for the source, and spotted her. A woman, not much older than me, sitting at a corner table, scribbling furiously in a notebook. The group at her table seemed oblivious to her or the song.

Frowning, I stepped closer. Something wasn't right. The air around her shimmered, and when she looked up, her gaze locked onto mine.

You see me, her lips mouthed the words, her eyes wide with a mix of excitement and desperation.

Before I could react, she floated—yes, floated—out of her chair and right up to me. My body froze, my mind screaming that this couldn't be happening.

"Help me," she whispered, her translucent hand gripping my arm. Her voice was a faint echo, but I felt the cold of her touch seep into my skin. "The angels sang me to sleep," she whispered, her voice fading like smoke. Then she flickered once and disappeared.

I stood there, staring at the empty space where she'd been, trembling. My brain scrambled for explanations, but there was no rationalizing what I'd just seen. *Ghosts. Real ghosts, and they're reaching out to me.*

Why? How? I needed answers, and there was only one person who had even hinted at them.

With shaking hands, I pulled Giles's business card from my bag, along with the map of the historic district. My skepticism was crumbling fast. I had to go to Monterey Square. Now.

As I walked, the memory of the café encounter replayed in my mind—the eerie hum, her cold hand gripping mine, her final whispered words. My heart raced as fear gripped my chest. *You're not losing your mind*, I told myself. But I needed someone to confirm that.

By the time I reached Monterey Square, I was running. My breath came in ragged gasps, and I barely noticed the clusters of tourists or the massive marble statue as I sprinted past. All I could think about was finding answers.

Finally, I spotted the address on a grand Georgian mansion, its white stone gleaming in the afternoon light. I slowed, taking deep breaths to calm myself as I walked through the wrought iron gate. This was it. Time to confront whatever this was and find out just how deep this rabbit hole went.

3

FILL IN THE BLANKS

Heart still racing from my frantic sprint, I hammered on the thick oak door, my breath coming in ragged gasps.

After a brief moment, it creaked open. Bushy eyebrows rose as Giles exclaimed. "Lenox! My word, you look like you've seen a ghost. What's happened?"

I shuddered. "Please, don't say that word."

Giles frowned. "What word?"

"Ghost. I've had more than enough of them this morning."

He blinked. "I think you'd better come in—no, on second thought, I feel sure your tale will be easier to recite once we've eaten."

Plopping his hat onto his head, he stepped over the threshold and pulled the door closed before offering his arm. "Shall we break our fast, my dear?"

Shaken from my ordeal and dazed by Giles's nonplussed reaction to my dramatic arrival at his home, I meekly let him guide me through the gate and across the square.

Fuchsia and white azaleas burst from every corner of the park, tourists snapping photos, captivated by the beauty of springtime in Savannah. I barely noticed. My mind was spinning, tangled in fear and confusion.

Giles set a gentle pace, his arm steadying mine as he filled the silence with easy, lighthearted chatter. He spoke of the weather and local gossip, his calm demeanor slowly loosening the knot of anxiety in my chest. But even with the serene surroundings and Giles's soothing voice, my mind kept drifting back to the ghostly figures I'd seen, pulling me into their shadowy grip.

As we exited the square, the rich aroma of fresh bread and brewing coffee filled the air, grounding me. The comforting smells, combined with Giles's steady presence, felt like a lifeline, tethering me to a fragile sense of normalcy.

I took a deep breath, letting the warmth of the sun and the steady rhythm of Giles's voice wash over me. By the time we crossed the street, the tight knot of fear in my chest had loosened, leaving behind a fragile calm.

Giles nodded toward a cozy corner café with a gentle smile. "Now then, let's get you something to eat, and you can tell me all about it."

La Paloma occupied the bottom floor of a historic building, its weathered brick façade adorned with intricately carved burgundy molding. The corner spot offered stunning views of the square through large windows framed with vibrant flower boxes overflowing with pansies.

As we neared the entrance, the warm, inviting aroma of coffee and spices made my mouth water. I hesitated at the threshold, my dwindling funds suddenly front and center. Panic flared—*could I even afford this meal?*

Giles, sensing my hesitation, gave my arm a reassuring squeeze. "Thank you for allowing me the honor of treating you to breakfast," he said with a grin. Eyes twinkling with laughter, he winked and gave my arm a gentle pat. "We'll refrain from mentioning the added benefit to my reputation for being seen in the company of such a lovely young woman, eh?"

His teasing broke through my anxiety, and I laughed. "Well, put that way, how can I refuse? I don't want to damage your street cred!"

"Just so," he chuckled, holding the door open with a sweeping gesture. "After you, my dear."

Temporarily freed from worrying about my finances, I relaxed and took in the surroundings as we waited to be seated. The interior was cozy—wood beams, heart pine floors, and rustic light fixtures cast a soft glow over framed art of historic Savannah and the nearby coastline. The low hum of conversation, clinking cutlery, and natural light pouring through the windows added to the warmth of the space.

"Good morning, Mr. Westlake! Right this way," the host greeted Giles like an old friend and led us to a table by the window. As we walked through the bistro, the cheerful bustle contrasted sharply with my earlier panic, helping the last of my tension melt away.

The server arrived promptly, taking our drink orders with friendly efficiency and mentioning that Marco, the owner, would stop by soon. The atmosphere felt comforting, a welcome change from the morning's chaos.

Giles lowered his menu and smiled. "If you enjoy pico de gallo made with tomatoes from just outside town and freshly made tortillas, I highly recommend Marco's huevos rancheros."

I glanced at the menu and shrugged. "Sure, why not? I don't know if I've ever had it, but I'm game to try." I suppressed a snort. *At this point, I'd eat anything not nailed down.*

While Giles placed our order, I took the opportunity to glance around. The mix of students, locals, and tourists, all laughing and enjoying their meals, with not a ghost in sight, let me relax a bit more.

I was watching a horse-drawn tour pass by the square when Giles leaned forward, propping his chin on his hand. "Lenox..." He mused. "Quite unique. I feel sure there's a story behind it." He smiled and cocked an eyebrow, waiting.

I snorted. *A story behind my name—what an understatement.* I hesitated for a moment, weighing how much to tell him, but in the end, what was the harm?

"There's definitely a story," I said with a rueful smile. "Since I don't remember my real one, I chose 'Lenox

Grady'—Lenox, after the mall parking lot where I was found half dead, and Grady for the hospital that saved me."

Giles's eyes widened in shock. "Half dead? That's quite severe. What happened, if you don't mind my asking?"

Shifting in my seat, I tried to ignore the familiar discomfort the memories—or lack thereof—always brought. "I don't know, really. I was found badly injured, mugged maybe? I was in a coma for a while. When I woke up, I had no memory of my life or who I was before that moment. They told me I died and had to be resuscitated." I shrugged. "That's about all I know."

Giles leaned back thoughtfully. "Died and resuscitated, you say? That's a traumatic experience. And you had no awareness of this...ability to see ghosts before then?"

"No, nothing," I replied, my voice tinged with growing frustration. "For all I know, I could have been a banker, a baker, or even a psychic before all this."

Giles steepled his fingers, lost in thought. "It's often said that near-death experiences can open doors—perceptual doors—that were previously closed. Perhaps your sensitivity to the spectral world developed as a result, or it awakened something latent within you."

His words hung in the air, and I couldn't help but turn them over in my mind. The idea that my near-death experience had unlocked something within me was both intriguing...and terrifying.

Giles nodded slowly. "That's quite a journey, Lenox. It must be incredibly difficult."

I appreciated his understanding and nodded. "It is, but I'm adjusting," I smirked. "Or I was until I got to Savannah and started seeing ghosts."

Giles offered a reassuring smile, patting my hand. "Thank you for sharing that with me. I promise, we'll find some answers together."

Just then, the server arrived with our food. I leaned back as he placed a steaming plate of huevos rancheros in front of me, the colorful medley of tomatoes and peppers making my mouth water. I sniffed and smiled at Giles. "This looks and smells amazing!"

Giles's eyes twinkled with pride. "It is! Marco's famous for his cooking." He gestured toward my plate. "Come, let's enjoy our meal and talk of lighter things, shall we?"

Grateful for the shift in tone, I nodded and dug into my food. As we ate, Giles steered the conversation to easier topics. I relaxed, answering his questions about my first impressions of the city while eagerly soaking up his wealth of knowledge about Savannah's history.

The waiter had just cleared our plates when I sat back, patting my stomach. "Ah, I'm so full! Thank you for a wonderful meal. And I love learning about the city. You make history come to life."

Giles smiled, a knowing glint in his eyes. "I'm glad you enjoyed it, and, after a fashion, you could say the past is very much alive." He held my gaze, his expression shifting from lighthearted to something more serious. "As I think you're beginning to realize..."

I stiffened, the lightness of our conversation fading as dread settled in. My mouth went dry. I sipped my water, trying to steady my nerves. *This is why you came to him—just say it!*

Giles cleared his throat, sensing my hesitation. I took a deep breath, forcing the words out. "I, uh, was out looking for work this morning and...well, something happened." I licked my lips, the memory of the ghost boy in the park flashing through my mind. "It sounds crazy—I mean, I can hardly believe it myself and I was there."

Giles tsked softly. "You are not crazy. Tell me what happened."

His steady gaze held no judgment, only concern. That simple reassurance was all I needed. The words tumbled out. "I ran into some...ghosts. One of them, she—"

My breath hitched as the memory of the café rushed back. I took a shaky breath. "There was a woman at the Quill and Brew..."

Giles nodded. "Go on."

I swallowed hard, biting my lip. "Okay. She, um...she was humming 'Moon River.' When our eyes met, she said, 'You see me,' and then...floated across the room. She grabbed my arm, asked me to help her, and then—" I hesitated, the memory still too surreal. "She started to fade. I could see right through her! She whispered something about...the angels singing her to sleep. And then she disappeared."

Giles leaned back, stroking his chin. "That must have been terrifying, Lenox. But it confirms what I suspected—you have a unique ability to connect with the past."

I stared at him, trying to shake off the unsettling images that my own words had conjured. My pulse quickened again as the weight of it all started to settle in.

Just then, a man approached our table, his broad smile cutting through the tension like a knife. I used the moment to take a deep breath and calm my nerves.

"Giles, my friend!" he exclaimed warmly. "And who's this lovely young lady?"

Giles grinned and gestured toward me. "Marco, this is Lenox. Lenox, meet Marco—the genius behind this fantastic meal."

I managed a small smile. "Thank you, it was wonderful."

Giles nodded. "Lenox was just telling me about her encounter with a ghost at the Quill and Brew this morning."

I grimaced and glanced at Marco, expecting ridicule. But instead, he simply smiled and said, "That's not uncommon in America's Most Haunted City."

"You don't think I'm crazy?" I blurted out.

"Not at all," Marco replied. "I don't think there's a square inch of this historic district that isn't haunted." He slid into the seat beside Giles, propping an elbow on the table. "And I worked at The Quill before I opened La Paloma. That place is definitely haunted."

I stared at him, wide-eyed. "You've, uh...you've seen them too?"

"Nah, wasn't that lucky," he chuckled, shaking his head. "But I've experienced some odd stuff. Footsteps when I was the only one there, doors opening and closing on their own, the smell of tobacco smoke when no one's smoking."

I gasped. "And you didn't run for your life?"

Marco shrugged. "You get used to it." Then he leaned forward, lowering his voice like he was about to share a secret. "So, tell me—what did this ghost look like?"

Astonished by his nonchalance, I hesitated before answering. "She had red hair and wore those round, granny glasses."

Marco frowned. "Red hair... How old do you think she was?"

I shrugged. "I don't know, do ghosts age?" I glanced at Giles, who shook his head.

"An interesting question. I've never seen a ghost but always assumed they retained their predeath appearance."

"Okay, well, she was kinda see through for most of the time, but I'd guess maybe early-thirties?"

Marco nodded. "And what was she doing in the café?"

"Well, humming 'Moon River' for one, but she was also sitting at a table, writing in a notebook."

Marco laughed. "Can't help you with the singing, but if she was sitting at the corner table to the left of the door then I might know who your ghost is."

My eyes widened. "Yes, she was sitting there, right by the window! Who do you think she is?"

He drummed his fingers on the table and frowned for a minute before answering. "Sounds like a journalist that lived above the coffee shop. I mean, it's been over a year since I worked there, but if she didn't move out, I'd say you saw Amelia Walsh." His expression fell and he shook his head.

"Didn't hear that she'd died though, sad if it's her. She was a talented writer and so young!"

My gaze dropped to the table as I thought of such a young, vibrant woman being cut down in her prime.

"Something wrong, Lenox?" Giles asked gently.

I took a deep breath, my gaze still fixed on the table. "It's just... she seemed so desperate. And excited that I could see her." I swallowed the lump forming in my throat. "I mean, what if she's been stuck in that café all this time, just waiting for someone to notice her?"

I shivered, remembering the sad way she hummed that melody. "And the way she was humming 'Moon River,' it wasn't just random. It was almost like a goodbye, you know? You think that song was playing when she died? Is that what she meant by angels singing her to sleep?"

Giles leaned back thoughtfully, stroking his chin. "It could be," he said, his voice soft with consideration. "But the more important question is why her spirit hasn't moved on. I suspect something in her life—or perhaps her death—remains unresolved."

He pulled out his phone and started typing. Without looking up he said, "You said Amelia Walsh, right Marco?"

"Yes but don't hold me to that. I'm just guessing."

Giles nodded and continued tapping his phone. After a minute or two he turned the screen toward me. "Is this who you encountered, Lenox?"

Smiling from the phone screen was a young woman with long auburn hair and warm brown eyes. I gasped. "Yes! That's her!" Giles had found an article in the local paper. "Does it say how she died?"

"Indeed,"" he said gravely. "It seems she was murdered and the case remains unsolved."

My stomach dropped. "Murdered? That's awful." I bit my lip, trying to process the information. "But why would she mention angels and 'Moon River'? And why is she still...lingering?"

Giles sighed, his voice gentle. "Many spirits linger when their deaths are unresolved. She might be waiting for someone to help her find peace. And finding someone who can actually see her? That's a rare opportunity she wouldn't pass up."

I swallowed hard, my throat tightening. "I can see that, I guess...but what am I supposed to do about it? I'm not exactly a detective. I mean"—I laughed, a little bitterly—"great. Seems like talking to ghosts is my only occupational skill. Not sure how that's going to pay the bills."

Giles cleared his throat. "About that...I may have a proposition."

I blinked. "A proposition?"

He smiled warmly. "Work for me as a tour guide. You've got the perfect...let's say, insider's perspective on Savannah's more ghostly citizens."

My eyes widened. "You're offering me a job?"

Giles nodded. Marco grinned, patting him on the back. "Best idea I've heard! You'll get the story straight from the source."

A shaky laugh bubbled up. "I don't know. I mean, I can't just summon ghosts at will. They come to me...I think."

"Exactly why this works," Marco chimed in. "Giles knows the history of the city's spirits better than anyone. He can help you figure out how to handle it."

Giles smiled, his eyes twinkling. "It's not charity, Lenox. I've been looking for help with my tours for a while. And your...unique talents will only make the experience more authentic."

He rattled off a salary that made my jaw drop. Then he added, almost casually, "And I have an apartment above my carriage house. The rent would be nominal, of course."

An offer too good to refuse—but hesitation still gnawed at me. What if I failed? What if I couldn't handle the ghosts or froze in front of tourists? But then again, what other options did I have?

Taking a deep breath, I met Giles's gaze. "You really think I can do this?"

"I do," Giles said confidently. "You've interacted with more spirits in a few days than most people do in a lifetime. That's no coincidence."

I bit my lip, considering. "And what exactly would I have to do?"

Giles chuckled. "You'll need to study a bit and take a short test to get your tour guide card—city requirements. After that, you'll simply lead our guests through Savannah's history, with a little help from your...connections."

"Take the job," Marco added with a grin. "You'll love it. And have you seen the Westlake Mansion?"

He stood up, giving me a playful wink. "Best get back to the kitchen. Great meeting you, Lenox. I expect to hear all about your ghostly adventures soon."

Bemused, I watched him walk away, feeling the weight of the morning lifting slightly. I'd woken up desperate and scared for my future, and now...

I flashed a grateful smile at Giles. "Thank you. Your offer couldn't have come at a better time."

He smiled back, rising to his feet. "No need to thank me. You've shown an interest in Savannah's history, and that's half the battle of being a good guide." His eyes twinkled. "And your gift will be invaluable."

As we left the bistro, a sense of purpose stirred within me. Maybe, just maybe, in helping these spirits, I'd uncover the keys to unlocking my own past—and forging a new future.

4

A HAUNTING EXPERIENCE

Well-dressed people mingle, their colorful outfits a striking contrast to the stark white walls. Servers offer champagne and canapés but I ignore them, navigating around the guests, my gaze fixed on a grouping of paintings at the back wall.

Standing before the paintings, I study the light and shadow on a river running through a marsh. Egrets hunt among the reeds, their white feathers so detailed my fingers itch to stroke them. In the middle ground stands a derelict cabin, its cedar planks weathered to dusty gray. The door and windows are painted blue, striking against the muted tones. A ramshackle dock stretches out, a dilapidated skiff bobbing at the end.

As I stare at the painting, a restless yearning stirs within me. There was something achingly familiar about the scene, a sense of *déjà vu that tugged at the edges of my memory. The cabin, hidden in the marsh, evoked a strange pull, stirring feelings I couldn't quite place. I could almost smell the briny marsh air and hear the distant call of a heron.*

I move my gaze to the second painting in the grouping, one depicting a maritime forest at night. The full moon looms in the sky, casting its glow over the landscape. A creek winds its way through the stand of pine and old forest growth, making its lazy journey to the ocean depicted in the background. In the distance, a bonfire flickers, sending tendrils of smoke up into the night.

Something is hovering at the edge of the forest. It's tall, slim, deep in shadow, but I get the impression it is a person. Leaning in to get a better look, a strange sensation washes over me. The room around me fades, and I'm drawn into the scene. The smell of wood smoke becomes real, burning my lungs as I breathe it in. The full moon's light intensifies, casting long, eerie shadows.

Suddenly, I'm running through the woods, the underbrush snagging at my gown. Panic grips my chest as I hear the shouts behind me. They're gaining on me! Torches flicker through the trees, casting menacing shadows that dance and twist.

I stumble and fall, the hem of my blue ballgown tangling around my feet. Gasping for breath, I lean against a tree, trying to calm my racing heart. Looking down, I see the golden snake embroidered on my skirt, its body winding around the fabric. The snake's eyes are emeralds, glowing with an otherworldly light. Mesmerized, I reach out a trembling hand toward them.

As my fingers hover over the snake's head, something startles me and the dream dissolves.

I woke up with a start, my heart pounding in my chest and my breaths coming in short gasps. The terror from the dream clung to me like a thick fog, my fingers still tingling as if I had really touched the snake's glowing eyes. The echoes of the shouts followed me out of the dream, making my skin crawl.

The terror felt too real to dismiss, and even awake, I couldn't shake the image of the serpent winding through the folds of my gown. Why did it feel so familiar?"

A sudden knock at the door jolted me fully awake, and my pulse quickened again. I blinked, disoriented for a moment, before I heard Giles's familiar voice.

"Lenox, are you in there?"

I dragged myself up from the sofa, still unsettled, the remnants of the dream clinging to my thoughts. Forcing myself to focus, I called out, "Just a second, Giles!"

I ran a hand over my face, trying to push the lingering fear aside as I moved to the door. Opening it, I found Giles standing there, his brow creased in concern.

"There you are, I was beginning to think you'd lost your nerve!" Giles stepped into my small living room, his usual cheerful demeanor undeterred.

He closed the door behind him and turned to face me, his expression shifting as he took in my appearance. His brow furrowed. "Are you feeling well, my dear? You seem paler than usual. There's nothing to fear about summoning a spirit, at least not this one."

I forced a smile, still feeling the edges of the nightmare pressing against my thoughts. I grabbed my jacket from the hook beside the door, trying to shake off the remnants of fear that clung to me.

"I'm fine. Just took a cat nap and I'm still groggy." I shrugged, trying to sound casual, but my heart hadn't fully slowed. "Don't worry, I'm not backing out. I can't wait to meet the captain."

The lie slipped from my lips easily enough, and it seemed to reassure Giles. He smiled, his eyes twinkling with excitement, and offered his arm. "Excellent! Shall we go?"

With no real choice but to follow, I looped my arm through his, letting him lead the way as we stepped out into the cool evening air.

We walked down St. Julian Street, the sun already below the horizon, leaving the city bathed in the pale glow of a crescent moon.

For over a month, I'd studied for my tour guide exam and learned more about my so-called gift. Despite Giles's unwavering confidence in my abilities, doubt still gnawed at me. I'd encountered Amelia Walsh's ghost, sure, but how was I supposed to help spirits find peace when I couldn't even piece together my own past?

Giles often spoke of spirits, hauntings, and the veil between worlds like they were as real as the ground beneath our feet. His belief was comforting in its certainty, but for me, each ghostly whisper felt like it was pulling me further from what I thought was real.

The truth was, I didn't know what to believe anymore. Had I always thought ghosts weren't real? Or was that just an assumption I made, filling in the gaps of a life I couldn't remember?

Without memories, how could I be sure of anything? My life had become a minefield of uncertainty, each step forward shadowed by a past I couldn't recall.

Naming myself had felt exhilarating, like I had a blank canvas to fill. But now, it only reminded me how little I knew about the person I used to be.

Amid the oscillating tides of belief in the supernatural, one small, resolute part of me whispered, *seek the truth, no matter how elusive or frightening.* It was that curiosity, not certainty, that kept me moving forward.

I glanced at Giles, reminded of all he'd done for me—and would continue to do. The past might be a void, but tomorrow was still a canvas, waiting for me to paint. And this time, I vowed, I'd create my own picture—no more uncertainty about whose life I was living.

Tonight would be my first deliberate attempt to summon a spirit. Giles had taught me about ghosts, how they manifested, and the different types, but I hadn't yet tested that knowledge. Until now.

Giles, a few steps ahead, paused and turned to me, his expression contemplative. Through narrowed eyes, he watched until I caught up. I offered a hesitant smile, and his features softened.

"There really is nothing to fear, Lenox. This is part of your journey." He gestured toward the quiet city street and the square just ahead. "Here, the past isn't just remembered; it's felt. Maybe, in learning to communicate with those who've left us, you'll find clues to your own."

I considered his words, but my hesitation wasn't about ghosts—it was about my slipping grip on reality. Still, I forced a smile. "You really think so? It seems farfetched."

I wasn't sure how conversing with the dead could help me uncover the missing pieces of my past, but stranger things were happening by the day. With each step into this spectral-tinged life, the impossible seemed more plausible.

The darkness deepened around us, heightening the whispers of history embedded in every brick and every leaf. Giles's words lingered in the air like a promise—or perhaps, a warning.

"Only the shadows know," Giles added with a chuckle, attempting to lighten the mood. "Now, should we be fortunate enough to encounter Captain Jonathon, remember to stay calm. Be polite. Remind him of his time on the high seas, compliment him... tell him..."

Giles continued talking, but my mind drifted. My thoughts circled back to the nightmares that plagued me and the gnawing anxiety over my sanity. Was this spectral world truly part of my life now, or was I losing my grip on reality?

Just as I began to berate myself, something caught my eye—a flash of gold against the dim light. I stopped in my tracks, squinting at a nearby brick wall. It wasn't the colorful graffiti that drew me in, but a wrought iron gate beside it.

Midway down the black metal pickets, a medallion gleamed—a serpent, intricately carved, its body curled in a perfect Ouroboros. Its eyes glowed a vivid sapphire blue, reflecting the faint light from the streetlamp.

A cold shiver ran down my spine. The symbol felt eerily familiar, as though it had been lurking on the edge of my consciousness for longer than just one nightmare.

Giles's chatter trailed off as he realized I wasn't beside him. He retraced his steps. "If you're not ready, we can always postpone—"

"No," I cut in, frowning as I pointed at the emblem. "That symbol. I've seen it before."

Giles turned his gaze to the medallion. His reaction was immediate—his breath hitched and his eyes narrowed, as if piecing together something I couldn't yet see.

"What is it?" I asked, my pulse quickening. The blue eyes of the serpent seemed to glow brighter, almost alive.

Giles stared at the emblem for a moment, his face paling. "You've seen this before?"

I nodded slowly. "Yes, in a nightmare, just before you picked me up tonight. The snake, the...Ouroboros."

He stayed quiet, his brow furrowing. "Do you know what it's for?" I pressed.

That's when his expression darkened. "It's...reminiscent of something I've come across before. But it was long ago—nothing you need to worry yourself with."

I frowned, my curiosity flaring. "Reminiscent of what?"

He hesitated, opening his mouth to speak, then seemed to think better of it, his voice growing tight. "Like I said—nothing you need to concern yourself with. Let's not keep Captain Harker waiting."

I opened my mouth to press Giles further, feeling that his reaction made a lie of his answer, but standing in the middle of the street arguing didn't seem like the wisest choice. Shrugging, I fell into step beside him, my mind still sifting through fragments of memory, trying to make sense of the serpent medallion.

We were approaching an old home that Giles declared was the Hampton-Lillibridge house when an icy draft swept down the street, bringing with it the distinct scent of decay—like something long dead, half-forgotten, but not at rest. The air seemed heavier here, dense with secrets and memories that hadn't seen daylight in years.

A shiver coursed down my spine, making me forget all about the strange medallion. My skin prickled with goosebumps as my earlier resolve flickered like a candle about to be snuffed out. The house loomed ahead, its darkened windows staring out like blind eyes, hiding whatever ghastly memories it held within.

Suddenly, the very atmosphere around us shifted. The air thickened, crackling with a dark energy that made every hair on the back of my neck stand on end.

My breath hitched, my lungs refusing to draw in air as the playful sense of exploration drained away, replaced by something far more sinister. Something was watching. Something from the shadows.

"Spirits are particularly strong here," Giles murmured, his voice barely a whisper as we neared the house.

The shadows deepened, swallowing what little light there was, as if the house itself was absorbing it. My heart thundered in my chest, a sudden oppressive weight pressing against me, tightening with every step.

"Giles, do you feel that?" I asked, my voice trembling, my eyes fixed on the black windows of the house. They stared back at me, unblinking and empty, like eyes that had seen too much.

Before Giles could respond, something lashed out from the darkness, an unseen force gripping me with cold, merciless fingers.

My breath seized in my throat, a crushing weight pressing against my chest, squeezing the air from my lungs. Panic flared as I stumbled back, my hands flying to my throat, but there was nothing to pull free.

"Giles!" I gasped, my voice little more than a strangled plea as the invisible force tightened its grip.

His eyes widened in alarm, and he lunged for me, grabbing my arm. "Focus, Lenox!" he urged, his voice urgent. "Remember what I told you about hostile spirits!"

Hostile spirits? I could barely think, let alone remember anything he'd said! The pressure around my throat became unbearable, darkness closing in at the edges of my vision as my lungs screamed for air. I gasped, clawing at the empty space, my strength slipping away.

"I. Can't. Breathe!" I managed to sputter as the force threatened to pull me under, drowning me in its icy grip.

Through the narrowing tunnel of my vision, I saw Giles spring into action. His hand dove into his messenger bag, pulling out something he scattered into the air. His voice, low and hurried, muttered an incantation, the words too fast for me to catch. The air shimmered, a strange ripple of energy crackling through the space between us.

Then, with an ear-splitting shriek, the force released me. I dropped to my knees, gasping for air, my chest heaving as I struggled to fill my lungs. My hands trembled as I pushed myself up. If this was a gift, I wanted to return it—preferably with a full refund.

Giles knelt beside me, his face pale but composed. "We need to leave," he said, his voice tight. "Now."

He didn't need to ask twice. I scrambled to my feet, clutching his arm for support as we hurried back the way we'd come. My legs felt like jelly, my lungs still burning, but the farther we got from the house, the more the oppressive weight lifted.

We stopped several blocks away, the air finally feeling lighter. My pulse slowed, though my body still trembled from the encounter. Giles watched me closely, concern etched into every line of his face. He rubbed my back as I sucked in deep breaths of the cool night air.

When I finally felt steady enough to speak, I glanced up at him. "I..." I began, my voice raspy. I swallowed hard, forcing the words out. "I'm okay. We can go on to—"

"We're not going back there tonight," Giles interrupted firmly, his tone leaving no room for argument. "You're not ready for that level of hostility yet. We need to get you some protection first." His decision was final, his concern palpable.

Relieved, I didn't argue. Protection sounded like the best idea I'd heard all night. After we'd put several more blocks between us and the violent spirit, my fear subsided enough to let curiosity creep back in.

"What...what was that back there?" I asked, my voice still shaky, but the question was burning in my mind.

Mouth pressed in a grim line, Giles responded, "That was the spirit of an angry old man who haunts the Hampton-Lillibridge house. You remember I told you about Mr. Williams, the antiques dealer who helped revitalize the historic district?"

I nodded, still catching my breath. "Yes, I remember you mentioning his trial for murder."

"Exactly. When Jim bought the house, he had it moved to its current location. During the renovations, workers reported strange occurrences—furniture moving on its own, knocks, bangs, cold spots...the usual things you hear about hauntings." He chuckled dryly. "It was just a curiosity at first. But when Jim moved in, he encountered that old spirit first-hand. After it tried to strangle him, Jim left the house and refused to speak of it again."

I shivered, the memory of the invisible hands around my throat still too fresh. "I thought you said spirits couldn't hurt people."

Giles sighed, his eyes serious. "Most of the time, they can't. But in rare cases, when a spirit is particularly angry or has a strong emotional connection to a place, they can manifest more aggressively. You handled yourself well tonight, Lenox. You stayed calm."

I let out a humorless laugh. "I didn't feel calm." I hesitated, then asked, "What was that flash of light? I saw dust in the air. Is that what stopped the attack?"

Giles nodded, nudging me to start walking again. "The dust you saw was iron filings. It's an old trick for dealing with hostile spirits. Iron disrupts their energy."

I blinked, trying to process that. "Iron filings?"

He chuckled softly. "There's still much you need to learn about the supernatural. But don't worry, we'll get you properly protected."

I frowned, following his pace as we crossed the street. "You've mentioned protection a few times. What exactly can protect someone from a ghost?"

He didn't answer right away, scanning the street ahead like he was on alert for more danger. I tensed, wondering if he sensed another attack, but after a moment, he seemed satisfied and resumed walking, pulling me along at a quicker pace.

The evening shadows deepened; the moon now hidden behind clouds. I felt the weight of the darkness pressing in, my senses still on high alert from the encounter. But Giles, ever calm, seemed unaffected by the oppressive night.

"Tomorrow, we'll visit Selena James's shop," he finally said, his voice cutting through the silence. "She's a skilled root worker, specializing in protective charms and spells. Selena will be able to craft something that will give you an edge in handling future encounters."

Relief washed over me at the idea of having something to defend myself. I nodded. "I want to be ready next time. I can't be terrified every time something like this happens."

Giles smiled approvingly. "That's the spirit, Lenox. With a bit of guidance, you'll be able to handle anything the supernatural throws at you. But for now, let's call it a night. You need to rest and recover."

As we headed back toward the heart of the city, the buzz of Savannah nightlife surrounded us, drawing me out of the eerie stillness I'd been trapped in. Tourists, students, and locals filled the sidewalks, their laughter and conversation a welcome return to normalcy. The strange world I'd just experienced slipped into the background, though I knew it was never far away.

Comfortable now that we were in a populated area, I let my thoughts drift and used the time to window shop. My first paycheck had finally hit my new bank account, but between everything happening, I hadn't found time to shop for clothes to fill my meager wardrobe or trinkets to personalize the carriage house apartment.

A boutique display caught my eye, but after seeing the prices, I resolved to stick with thrift stores. I was employed, but that didn't mean I had money to burn!

"Lenox, did I ever tell you about the time one of my tour guests swore she'd seen a spirit?" Giles chuckled, amused at the memory. "She claimed she'd been possessed! Too much late-night television, no doubt…"

I half-listened as Giles continued his tale, but my pace slowed as we neared a window filled with artwork. A gilded frame caught my eye, the painting inside drawing me in with its image of a river bathed in moonlight.

The scene pulled at me, its gentle current almost beckoning. I smiled, shaking off the fanciful thought, and noticed the gallery's name: Clarke's Fine Art Gallery. Just down the street from the Westlake Mansion. I made a mental note to stop in next time.

We were walking past Bennet's Books when something flickered in the second-story window. The light inside shimmered strangely, like sunlight rippling over water.

I blinked, sure my eyes were playing tricks, but the flicker remained. It was as if the window was a thin veil, and something on the other side was trying to break through.

My heart stuttered in my chest. "Did you see that?" I whispered, rooted to the spot, my eyes locked on the window. A strange, cold pull tugged at me, urging me to step closer.

Giles stopped, following my gaze. "See what?" he asked, his voice low, calm.

"Up there...the light, it was flickering, like something was trying to break through." I pointed, my pulse quickening.

Giles studied the window, but by the time his eyes fixed on it, the flickering light had vanished. The window now looked perfectly ordinary, revealing only the quiet, empty apartment above the bookstore. The strange distortion, the rippling air—it was gone, as if it had never been there.

I swallowed hard, my throat suddenly dry. "It was right there..." I whispered, my voice trailing off, unsure if I'd imagined it.

Giles kept his gaze on the window a moment longer, then glanced back at me. "Eloise Bennet doesn't live on the premises, and she hasn't had a tenant in the apartment for over a year. I'll give her a call, but she has a sound security system."

I hesitated, still feeling the lingering unease from what I'd just seen—or thought I'd seen. "Maybe it's just my nerves," I muttered, trying to shake off the feeling. "But I could've sworn..."

Giles nodded, gently tipping his head in a silent request to keep walking. "It's likely your mind is still reeling from earlier. This is a good reminder—we're not just dealing with what's in front of us. These spirits, they're part of Savannah's fabric, woven into every building, every street."

I nodded, trying to steady my breathing as I walked beside him. The idea of encountering another ghost was unsettling, but a small part of me was intrigued. Was every building in the historic district haunted? Did every ghost have a story to tell?

I glanced back at the window once more, half-expecting to see the flicker return, but it remained dark and still. Maybe Giles was right. Maybe it was just my mind playing tricks on me.

But the feeling lingered, like a ripple that hadn't fully settled. Yet that strange pull, the warmth in my chest...that was real. And the sense that whatever had just happened wasn't over lingered, refusing to fade.

Even as I tried to brush it off, the flickering light in Bennet's Books nagged at me. It wasn't like the violent energy we'd felt outside the Hampton-Lillibridge house—this was something subtler, almost like an invitation. It tugged at me, tempting me to dig deeper, to uncover whatever was lurking behind that glass.

Still, some things were better left unexplored. I shuddered, remembering the violent encounter we'd just escaped. No thank you! Apparently, I needed a reminder that curiosity killed the cat.

A cheeky voice in my head shot back, *but satisfaction brought it back!*

Yeah, but a cat has nine lives and I'm not a cat! I thought, mentally giving that snarky voice the middle finger.

Shaking off my ridiculous inner argument, I focused back on what Giles was saying, though the nagging feeling refused to fade completely.

"We will explore further," Giles assured me as we crossed Monterey Square. "For now, rest. We'll visit Selena tomorrow, and you'll need your strength. Protective charms are just the beginning, Lenox. We're going to need them if you're to face the shadows waiting in places like the Quill and Brew."

The promise of deeper secrets mingling with the tangible history of Savannah hung between us as we parted ways in Giles's garden.

I opened the old oak door to the carriage house, eager for a quiet night on the sofa with a cup of tea and another chapter of the Savannah history book Giles had loaned me. I stepped inside, the comforting smell of worn leather and old wood easing my nerves.

I closed and locked the door, glad to leave the shadows behind. For now.

5

ROOTS RUN DEEP

True to his word, Giles rousted me from bed early the next morning, insisting it was essential I get protection from vengeful spirits before I started conducting tours by myself. He'd get no argument from me, regardless of how much I loved sleeping in!

We walked across the square, passing Marco's bistro, La Paloma, before turning into a narrow alley that opened up to reveal a quaint shop front, its windows and door trimmed in vivid blue. The sign above the door read: The Rooted Spirit Apothecary.

As we neared the entrance, my nose twitched from the earthy smells of herbs mingling with the heady aroma of the jasmine vine climbing up the weathered brick facade. The door was propped open, inviting us inside.

"Here we are," Giles announced, gesturing for me to enter first.

Stepping inside, I was enveloped by the scent of sage, lavender, and other spices I couldn't name. The shop was a cozy cavern of wonders, with shelves stocked full of jars and bottles, bundles of dried herbs hanging from the ceiling, and roots and natural curiosities displayed in glass cases. The heart pine floors added to the rustic charm.

A bell tinkled as Giles drew the door closed, drawing the attention of a woman who emerged from behind a curtain at the back of the shop. She was a striking figure, her skin a deep mahogany and her hair styled in an intricate pattern of braids and beads. Her presence was commanding yet warm, and her brown eyes twinkled with a knowing light.

She handed something wrapped in brown paper to a man standing at the counter and then turned toward us as he inspected his purchase.

"Good mornin', Giles," she greeted with a lilted accent that sang of the Georgia coast. "And who's this ya brought me?"

"This is Lenox Grady," Giles introduced. "Lenox, meet Selena James, Savannah's finest root worker."

Selena's customer handed her a few bills. As she put them in the cash register, the man turned, nodded at Giles, and then glanced at me. His eyes widened slightly, and he quirked an eyebrow at Giles, smirking. "Keeping secrets, Giles?"

Giles's jaw tightened, but he remained silent. The man chuckled softly and turned to leave.

He couldn't have been much older than me, but he had an air of command that belied youth. Tall, with wavy brown hair and piercing blue eyes, he was almost too handsome.

I tried not to stare, but as he brushed past me, our eyes locked, and a strange thrill shot through me. He noticed, and a devilish smile tugged at his lips. "See you soon...*Little Spark.*"

My eyes widened. "Wha—" My response fell on deaf ears as he strolled out of the shop.

I turned, about to ask Giles what that had been about and who the man was, but Selena came around the counter. Before I could gather my scattered wits, she was taking my hand.

"Mmm, I see. The spirits been talkin' to ya, ain't they, chile?"

I blinked, taken aback. "How did you—"

Selena chuckled softly. "Don't need no introduction to know that, honey. Your aura shines like a new penny. You got a gift, whether you ready for it or not."

Giles nodded at me, as if to confirm Selena's words. "We were hoping you might help Lenox with some protection. She's had a few...encounters already."

"Ah, I thought as much," Selena said, moving to one of her shelves. She began selecting various items—a small pouch, a vial of oil, and a bundle of what looked like dried herbs tied with a blue ribbon. "Now, Lenox honey, what you need is a little sometin' to shield ya from those who might mean ya harm, spirit or otherwise."

As Selena gathered the items, my gaze wandered around the shop, taking in the mystical and intriguing contents. It was a lot to take in, this new reality of ghosts and magic. But even as Selena talked, my thoughts kept drifting back to that man—the stranger from earlier.

See you soon.

The way his eyes had lingered on mine, the strange, electric pull I'd felt when we made eye contact. It was unsettling, and yet... something about it left me wanting to know more. Why had his words stuck with me? And what had he meant by soon, and why did he call me Little Spark?

"Now, here's what I got for ya," Selena said, returning with her hands full. I shook off the lingering thoughts of the stranger and focused.

"Dis here is a mojo bag—keep it on ya at all times." She handed me a small leather pouch. "Inside is angelica root, salt from the marshes, and a piece of quartz. It'll help keep da spirits from gettin' too close."

Next, she handed over a vial. "Anoint yourself with this oil at sunrise. It'll cleanse your aura." Selena clapped her hands. "Now, ya need a talisman. Come dis way..."

As I followed Selena through the aromatic aisles of the apothecary, my gaze was drawn to a small, dimly lit corner where a variety of stones glittered under a single beam of light. Selena paused, her hands hovering above the collection of crystals.

"Now, for ya protection, we need a stone dat resonates with ya spirit," Selena began, her voice a soothing hum. She picked up a black stone, not much bigger than a quarter. Its surface was shiny and smooth and it seemed to absorb the light around it.

"Dis here is black tourmaline. It's powerful for protection, especially against spiritual negativity. It'll ground ya, keep ya safe from da spirits who might wish ya harm."

Selena placed the stone on my palm, urging me to close my fingers around it. "Feel dat?"

My eyes widened as a slow, pulsing vibration spread from the stone, making my palm warm. I gawped at Selena.

She grinned, flashing pearly white teeth. "Ah, knew ya had da power in ya." She nodded toward my palm. "Dat's the stone speaking to ya. It's choosing ya as much as you is choosing it."

I stared at my hand, fascinated by the power thrumming through the cool, black stone. "That's...incredible!"

"Ah, dat it is." Selena pulled a pair of white cotton gloves from her apron pocket. Once she'd pulled them on, she lifted the stone from my hand and tipped her head indicating I should follow her to a small table set up with various oils, herbs, and candles in a rainbow of colors.

She selected a small bottle of oil. "Dis is infused with rosemary and sage for purification and protection." Uncorking the bottle, she used a dropper to gently anoint the black tourmaline, murmuring words in a flowing, rhythmic cadence.

"This oil, blessed by da moon and sung over with prayers, will bind the stone's protection to ya. As I anoint dis tourmaline, so are you shielded from harm," Selena intoned. The rich, earthy scent of the oil filled the air, mingling with the sharper fragrances of the shop.

I watched, fascinated. "Selena, Giles said you were a root worker. What exactly is that?"

Selena looked up, a smile crinkling the corners of her eyes. "Ah, root work is part of da hoodoo, chile, a sacred tradition. It's not just about spells and magic, though that's part of it. It's about connecting deeply with da roots of da earth, da spirits of da ancestors, and da energies that move through all things."

Selena continued, walking over to a shelf filled with various roots, herbs, and bottles. "Take dis here John de Conqueror root," she picked up a small, knobby root and held it out for me to see. "It's used for strength and overcoming obstacles. People carry a piece of it in dey pocket when dey need to face a tough situation or challenge."

I reached out, touching the root with a sense of reverence. "So, it's like...having a piece of protective energy with you?"

"Exactly!" Selena placed the root back on the shelf. "And over here"—she moved to another part of the shop where jars filled with various colored contents lined the wall—"we have honey jars. These are used for sweetening someone's feelings toward you—be it for love, favor, or smoothing over conflicts."

Selena picked up a small, honey-filled jar with herbs floating within it. "By placing personal items or names in the jar and performing a ritual, you set your intentions into motion. It's about putting your will out dere, in alignment with da natural energies."

"That sounds powerful...and a bit daunting." My gaze followed Selena as she put the jar away.

"It can be, chile. But dat's why it's important to approach these practices with respect and understanding." Selena's tone grew serious, her eyes meeting mine. "Root work and hoodoo ain't just about changing ya external circumstances;

they about transformation, inner growth, and respecting da balance of the world around us."

I bit my lip and nodded slowly, absorbing the weight of Selena's words. "And these practices, they help people connect with that power?"

"Dat's right," Selena affirmed, her voice soft but emphatic. "They empower us to take active roles in our spiritual and physical lives. It's about healing, protecting, and sometimes, yes, even guiding lost spirits, like those ya have encountered."

My thoughts drifted to the ghost of Amelia Walsh. "I see. It's all connected then—the spirit world and our own, through these practices."

Selena smiled warmly, pleased with my understanding. "Ya catch on quick. Remember, every root, every herb, every ritual has its place and purpose. If ya ever in doubt, ya come see me. We'll figure it out together."

"Thank you, Selena. I think I'm going to need all the help I can get."

Selena chuckled. "Dat's what I'm here for. Now, let's get dat talisman finished. Ya got a whole new world to explore, and I'll make sure ya ready for it."

Selena returned to her work table and picked up a spool of copper wire. She carefully wound it around the stone, fashioning a loop to hang from a chain. "In da hoodoo, we use the materials the earth gives us—roots, stones, bones. We speak to spirits, and yes, we make charms and potions. But all of it, every bit, is grounded in deep respect for nature and for those who came before us."

She handed the finished pendant to me. "Dis here is more than just a stone on a string. It's a symbol of ya connection to da larger world, to da protective spirits, and to da heart of hoodoo itself."

I slipped the pendant over my head, feeling its weight as both a physical and spiritual anchor as it nestled between my breasts. It sounded crazy, but I immediately felt safer.

Considering what I was about to do, I needed it. I hadn't told Giles yet, but I couldn't stop thinking about Amelia Walsh and her mournful song.

She'd been surprised and then relieved when she realized I could see her, and that had to mean something. What, I wasn't sure, but since she'd whispered that the angels sang her to sleep three times, it seemed like she was trying to tell me something. What that was remained to be seen, but if my ability was a gift as Giles suggested, then I should use it to help—and that meant seeking out Amelia Walsh's spirit.

I fingered the black stone and smiled. "Thank you, Selena. I think I'm starting to understand, not just hoodoo, but what I'm meant to do."

Selena nodded, pleased. "Ya keep dat mind open, Lenox. It'll serve ya well as ya walk dis path." Her eyes twinkled. "And remember, ya always welcome here. The Rooted Spirit ain't just a shop; it's a sanctuary."

I picked up the other items, feeling the weight of responsibility that came with them. "Thank you again, Selena."

Remembering my encounter outside the Hampton-Lillibridge house, I swallowed hard. "Um, but, what if I need more? What if this isn't enough?"

Selena studied me for a long moment before nodding slowly. "Chile, if you find ya need more, ya come back here. I'll teach ya about da root and hoodoo. But for now, start with these. They'll guide ya well."

I had started to turn away when Selena touched my arm.

"Lenox, I sense many things about ya are still to be discovered, but for now, just remember, you are more powerful than ya know."

As we left the shop, Giles placed a reassuring hand on my shoulder. "You're doing well, Lenox. It's a lot to take in, but I believe you're on the right path."

Looking back at the apothecary shop, its blue trim bright against the brick, I fingered the pendant and considered all that Selena had told me, especially her parting words. *More powerful?* Did I even want to know what that meant?

6
SECRETS REVEALED

The evening air was filled with the heady scent of magnolia, and a cool breeze hinted at the spectral presence the old city welcomed after sundown.

I stood at the gates of Colonial Park Cemetery, the soft glow of my lantern casting deep shadows on the cobblestones beneath my feet as I prepared to conduct my first solo ghost tour.

With everyone assembled, I surreptitiously glanced at my notes and faced my audience. "As we walk these haunted grounds"—my voice was surprisingly steady considering the butterflies in my stomach—"keep your eyes and ears open. Savannah is a city of the dead as much as it is of the living."

I pointed to the looming gates behind me, their iron bars seeming to twist and writhe in the lantern's glow. "Welcome to Colonial Park Cemetery. While the gates are locked at dusk, trapping the spirits within, our journey tonight will unveil the haunted secrets that linger just beyond this fence."

As I stepped up to the gates, a sudden draft brushed against my skin—a cold whisper from the shadows of the night, prickling the hairs on the back of my neck.

My heart raced at the thought of encountering a ghost mid-tour. The protective talisman rested solidly against my chest, a constant reminder of the dangers lurking in the shadows. Would Selena's charms be enough to shield me? The uncertainty gnawed at me, but I forced a smile for my audience.

Despite my newfound abilities and knowledge, there was a part of me that remained apprehensive about facing the spirits of Colonial Park alone in the dark.

With a deep, steadying breath, I pushed these fears aside, reminding myself of Giles's reassurances and the black tourmaline stone hanging around my neck. The last of the group had arrived; it was show time.

"Colonial Park Cemetery is considered one of the most haunted places in Savannah. Opened in 1750, it is the oldest burial ground in Savannah to remain intact. While there are a few burial sites used prior to 1750, those have all been covered up, built on top of, or paved over." I waved my lantern, casting light on the pavement beneath our feet. "This habit of building over the dead has earned Savannah a rather unsettling title—the City That Lives Upon Her Dead."

I grinned as the group glanced down at their feet, their eyes filled with both intrigue and trepidation. "With every step you take in Savannah, odds are good you are literally walking on the bones of our ancestors."

"Speaking of ancestors, there is one I'd rather not meet." My voice dropped to a hush as I gathered the group closer around the flickering light of my lantern.

"One of the most notorious spirits said to haunt these grounds is that of Rene Rondolier," I began, my eyes scanning the faces in the group. I paused, letting the silence stretch, building anticipation. "Rene was a figure cloaked in mystery and darkness, a man whose life story is as murky as the mist that rolls off the Savannah River at dawn." I glanced at the cemetery gates, stillness amplifying my words.

I let the imagery sink in, then continued. "In the early 1800s, Rene was known throughout Savannah for his towering height and gaunt, intimidating presence. But it was not just his appearance that frightened the locals—it was the rumors that swirled around him. It was whispered that he was responsible for the disappearance of several townsfolk, and even more terrifying, children who ventured into the cemetery where Rene liked to play."

The group shifted uneasily, the flicker of the lantern casting ghostly shadows across their faces. I lowered my voice to a near whisper, making the group lean in to catch every word. "One foggy evening, after another child went missing, the townspeople reached their breaking point. A mob formed and went in search of Rene, finding him under the light of the full moon in this very cemetery."

I directed my lantern light so that it swept over a nearby cluster of old, weathered tombstones. "They found him digging in the earth, right here among these graves. The mob, fueled by fear and rage, never gave him a chance to explain.

He was taken from this place and hanged from the largest oak tree in Wright's Square. Rene's final screams cursed the town, vowing that his spirit would never rest, nor would the town know peace."

Turning, I pointed toward the winding paths that meandered through the cemetery. "To this day, visitors report seeing the shadow of a tall figure, roaming the grounds, and some hear the whispers of Rene's curse in the wind. They say he's still searching, perhaps for his own justice, or maybe for new souls to take with him."

The group stared, caught between horror and fascination, as the night's sounds seemed to echo Rene's restless wanderings. I watched their rapt faces, knowing I had them hooked. "Keep close," I said with a slight smile, "we wouldn't want anyone to wander off and encounter Rene alone, would we?"

I let them look through the cemetery fence while I mentioned a few historical figures buried inside, along with duels fought beneath the live oaks, and finished with tales of voodoo workers robbing graves.

Once the group had looked its fill, I guided them along Abercorn Street. The grand facade of The Cathedral Basilica of St. John the Baptist loomed ahead, its steeple piercing the night sky. Reaching the steps of the church, I waited for the group to gather round.

"This magnificent structure is not just a sanctuary of faith but of spirits," I continued, my voice echoing slightly off the cathedral's large oak doors. "One spirit, a former priest named Father O'Reilly, is said to appear during the hour of compline, praying fervently at the altar before vanishing at the stroke of midnight."

Murmurs rippled through the group, some glancing nervously at the darkened windows, half-expecting a glimpse of the praying priest.

The tour continued, with me filling the time between stops with chatter and curious facts about the city. As we approached Lafayette Square, my lantern light flickered mysteriously, casting ghostly shadows.

"This square," I said, pausing to ensure everyone could hear me, "is haunted by the laughter of children long gone." I pointed toward a grand house overlooking the green park. "That's the Hamilton-Turner Inn. It's thought the ghostly children lived in the house when it was the private residence of Samuel Hamilton."

I stepped off the path, the crisp crunch of dried leaves underfoot mingling with the distant hoot of an owl, the air thick with the scent of damp earth and decaying foliage. Raising my lantern a bit higher, I let its light cast dramatic shadows on the facade of the Hamilton-Turner Inn.

"Guests have reported hearing the sounds of billiard balls rolling across the floor late at night." I kept my voice low hoping it added to the mystery. Giles was right. Being a ghost tour guide was part historian and part actor and I was totally getting into my role.

I'd studied enough to be proficient in the city's history but hadn't been sure I could pull off the dramatic flair Giles achieved so effortlessly. Glancing at the intrigued expressions on my audience's faces, I could lay that fear to rest; I had them eating out of my hand.

Letting the lantern illuminate my face, I arched a brow and added, "Imagine being alone in that grand old house, hearing the echo of a game played by invisible players."

Smiling at the nervous looks on several faces, I turned slightly, pointing upward toward the roof. "And then, there's the man on the roof. He's often seen late at night, silently smoking his cigar as he watches over the square. Some say he is Samuel Hamilton himself, keeping an eye on his former home from his favorite spot."

I let the silence hang for a moment, allowing the images I had painted sink deep into their imaginations. "It's these stories and more that weave the rich tapestry of Savannah's ghostly history. Each echo of laughter or sight of a spectral figure adds another layer to our understanding of the past—a past that never quite leaves us. Shall we move on?"

The group eagerly followed me as we made our way down Charlton Street, pausing outside the Gordon-Low house for another spooky tale about the founder of the Girl Scouts.

With each story, I was more anchored to the spectral world. To my audience, ghosts were just stories, meant to titillate, but I knew there was much more lurking in the shadows.

We crossed into Madison Square, the air growing noticeably cooler. The flickering lantern light cast elongated shadows that danced eerily across the weathered brick paths.

I slowed my pace as we approached the imposing statue of Sergeant William Jasper, a Revolutionary War hero whose stern visage seemed to watch over the square with a silent, solemn vigilance.

"This square," I began, "is not just known for its historical monuments, but also for its restless spirits."

I paused, glancing around as if to make sure we were alone. "One spirit, in particular, is said to linger near this very statue. They call him the weeping soldier. On nights like this, some have seen him, a figure in Revolutionary War attire, his face sorrowful as he gazes upon the statue of Sergeant Jasper."

I glanced at the statue and sucked in a breath. Standing beside the monument was a young man dressed in a colonial uniform, just as I'd described. He stared at me, his expression a haunting blend of sorrow and longing that made my breath catch.

My heart pounded as I met the ghost's eyes, my body freezing with fear. I desperately shook my head, willing him to understand that now was not the time for a conversation.

He stared a second longer and then faded into the night. A peak at my group showed they saw nothing out of the ordinary. I let out a breath I hadn't realized I was holding.

"Legend has it," I continued, "the weeping soldier was a friend of Jasper, who died in the Siege of Savannah, right here where we stand. Overwhelmed with grief and unable to leave the site of such personal tragedy, his spirit remains, forever mourning his friend and the futility of war."

The group leaned in, hanging on my words, oblivious to my brief moment of fear. Their excitement was contagious, stirring something in me, though the nervous tension still hovered at the edge of my mind. These spirits were real to me now, more than just stories to entertain tourists.

I made a mental note to come back to Madison Square when I could safely speak with what I was sure was the ghostly friend of Sergeant Jasper. This was my world now, and I was its voice.

I got back into my role and led the group down Bull Street and into the Crescent Moon Pub. Inside, surrounded by the warm glow of antique lanterns and the murmur of other patrons, I gathered my group around the fireplace.

"Our next story," I began, raising my voice slightly to be heard of over the patrons, "concerns a gambler known as Sly-eyed Sam, whose luck famously ran out right where you're standing." I warily glanced up at the balcony hoping the gambler's ghost wouldn't put in another appearance.

"He was caught cheating at cards and met his untimely end up on that balcony." I held my breath, watching for signs my recitation had summoned the spirit as the group chuckled nervously.

When all remained quiet in the spirit world, I relaxed and entertained the audience with another ghostly tale while they finished their drinks. As the crowd began to file out of the pub, buoyed by the spirits both told and drunk, I moved ahead to lead them to their next stop.

I was passing the Quill and Brew coffee shop when an unmistakable drop in temperature washed over me. Pausing, my hand clutching the pendant under my shirt for reassurance, I turned to face the café.

The streetlamp flickered ominously as the air grew colder, and then I saw her—Amelia Walsh, manifesting faintly against the dim light, her expression sorrowful and pleading.

My heart raced as Amelia's ghostly form solidified, her voice a haunting melody that sent a wave of unease through me. "Moon River" echoed through the night, a spectral lullaby filled with sorrow and desperation.

"Help me," Amelia whispered, the words barely audible over the breeze.

I glanced nervously toward my group; they were approaching fast and would be within earshot in seconds. Looking at Amelia, I whispered, "I want to help, but I can't talk right now. Can you meet me here later?"

Amelia's form flickered, her presence weakening as she murmured cryptically, "The angels sang me to sleep with that song."

The moment was broken as the group approached, their voices pulling me back from the spectral encounter. Forcing a smile, I impulsively turned to my audience.

"This very spot," I said, gesturing to the coffee shop, "is haunted by poor Amelia Walsh, a journalist tragically murdered a few years ago. The case remains unsolved to this day. They say she continues her daily routine of writing at the corner table"—I nodded toward the café window—"and she hums the song 'Moon River,' because it was playing as her life slipped away."

A tall man at the back of the group gasped when I mentioned the song. I glanced at him, startled by the intensity of his expression. His dark eyes glared at me with suspicion and anger.

As we made our way toward Monterey Square, the feeling of being watched persisted, prickling at the back of my neck. Every instinct screamed at me to turn around.

When I finally stole a glance back, the man had isolated himself from the group, speaking in hushed, urgent tones into his phone. His brow remained furrowed; his dark, piercing gaze locked onto mine, as though he could strip away my defenses and uncover truths I wasn't even aware of.

I managed a shaky smile and struggled to maintain my composure as I concluded the tour with a brief tale about the famed antiques dealer and star of the book and movie, *Midnight in the Garden of Good and Evil*. But the man's scrutinizing eyes never wavered, pressing down on me like a suffocating weight.

The group dispersed and under the dim glow of the street lamps, I crossed the square and approached the gate leading to the Westlake Mansion. The sensation of being watched clung to me. Hand on the brass doorknob, I turned and caught my breath. Arms crossed over his chest, the man stood in Monterey Square, watching me intently.

His dark eyes had followed my every move, and a sinking suspicion gnawed at me—our paths were destined to cross again, and I feared what that might bring.

7
GHOSTS OF THE PAST

Buzzing with excitement over the success of my first solo tour, I tidied up the small living room of the carriage house and contemplated how to spend the day. Since tours didn't start until ten p.m., I had hours to kill, and shopping sounded like a great idea.

I was putting my lantern back on its hook, considering where to start spending money, when a sharp knock at the door startled me. Expecting Giles, I smiled and opened the door but immediately sucked in a breath at the sight of my visitor.

The man who'd stared at me during the tour last night was now standing on my doorstep, glaring at me again. Fighting the urge to slam the door in his face, I closed it halfway and forced a polite smile. "Yes? How can I help you?" I asked, my voice betraying a hint of unease.

The man flashed a badge, his steel-blue eyes cold and un-relenting. "Detective Derek Vance. I need to talk to you about last night's tour. Specifically, the murder of Amelia Walsh."

My eyes widened, and I fought to keep my heart rate steady. "Um, I think there's been a misunderstanding. I use stories that are well-known around here."

Vance's stare hardened. "Miss Grady, that's not a well-known story. I think you'd better come with me to the station."

I swallowed hard as my knees threatened to buckle. What was going on? A million thoughts raced through my mind. "Can I call my employer first? He should know where I am."

Vance nodded, his patience wearing thin. "Make it quick."

I dialed Giles, who reassured me. "Go with him, Lenox. I'll contact my attorney just in case, but I'm sure it'll be fine. Stick to the truth without revealing too much about your abilities."

Taking a deep breath for courage, I hung up the phone. "Okay, Detective Vance. I'll come with you."

The interrogation room in the police station was a stark, fluorescent-lit space that made me long for the ghostly shadows of Savannah's streets. Detective Derek Vance sat across from me, his broad shoulders and stern features imposing against the dull gray walls. His sharp, cold eyes seemed to strip away my defenses, making me feel more exposed than I had in front of any ghost.

Detective Vance placed a recorder on the table between us and clicked it on, his gaze never leaving mine. "Ms. Grady," he began, his tone measured, "last night during your tour, you mentioned 'Moon River' was playing when Amelia Walsh was found dead. That's a detail we never released to the public. How exactly did you come to know about it?"

Oh crap! My stomach tightened. I hadn't realized that the tragic melody Amelia shared with me wasn't public knowledge! "Detective, I—"

Vance leaned forward, interrupting me. "It's a very specific piece of information, Ms. Grady. One that could only be known by someone involved in the investigation or..." He trailed off, his implication clear and ominous.

A cold draft whispered through the room, and I shivered, feeling the familiar unease of an unseen presence. I stroked my protective pendant and fought to keep my voice steady. "I can explain," I said, my voice wavering slightly under his scrutiny.

"Please do," Vance said, leaning back, arms folded across his chest.

I took a deep breath, the temperature dropping as a whisper of ethereal energy swirled through the room. "I communicate with spirits," I admitted, my voice barely above a whisper. "Amelia's spirit spoke to me."

Vance's eyebrows shot up, skepticism clear on his face. "You're saying that you talk to dead people?"

As if on cue, the cold intensified, and a faint voice whispered to me.

Hovering next to Vance's chair was a young girl, she couldn't have been more than eight or nine. I smiled, and her lips spread into a grin that lit her cornflower blue eyes. She giggled and waved. Conscious of Vance's scrutiny, I refrained from responding, but the little girl didn't seem to mind.

Trying to focus on the detective, I shifted in my chair, but the little ghost girl simply floated across the table to perch beside me, her legs dangling over the side.

"Hi, I'm Emily." She turned her head and looked at Vance. "He can't see me, why can you?"

"Ms. Grady?" Vance cleared his throat. "You're claiming that the ghost of the murder victim spoke to you." He snorted. "That's your story? That you're psychic?"

I bit my lip, glancing between Emily and the scowling detective, unsure who to answer first.

"Uh..." I swallowed hard and glanced at Vance. His jaw was tight, and his eyes were as cold and hard as steel. Talking to him about my abilities would be like shouting at a brick wall. I shrugged and went with the easier option.

"Hi, I'm Lenox." I smiled as Emily started swinging her legs, not a care in the world. "He can't see you because most people can't see spirits. I have a gift..."

Her expression fell. "Oh." She stared at the table, drawing little circles with her finger. "I really need to talk to him."

"Ms. Grady." Vance rolled his eyes. "Pretending to talk to the air isn't going to get you out of this." He slapped his palms on the table, making me jump. "Now, what do you know about the murder of Amelia Walsh?"

I licked my lips. "I, uh, told you. I don't know anything other than that she thinks the angels sang her to sleep and hums 'Moon River,' which is why I assumed it was playing when she died."

I leaned forward, determined to make him understand. "Look, talking to ghosts...they don't always make sense. I'm new to this, but I think it must take a lot of energy for them to contact me, so what they say is often broken sentences and stuff."

Vance scoffed and sat back in his chair, arms crossed over his chest. Giving up, I glanced at Emily. What I'd said about energy must have been true because my little friend was starting to fade.

She'd looked so sad when I explained why Vance couldn't see her, and I recalled her saying she really needed to talk to him...

"Emily, what did you need to tell him?"

Vance gasped. "Emily?" His voice was a harsh whisper.

Glancing at him, I noticed he'd paled. His lips were pressed into a tight line, and a nerve ticked in his cheek.

"Yes, do you know her?" Flickering light drew my attention. Emily was fading fast.

"Emily, what do you want me to tell him?"

"Stop this!" Vance shot up from his chair so fast it crashed to the floor. "How do you know that name? Emily is my sister. She... she's been missing since we were kids."

Emily was talking, so I ignored Vance's question, though my heart was breaking for him. "Say it again, Emily. I can hardly hear you."

A whisper, softer than a summer breeze, reached my ears, and then Emily was gone. Sighing, I looked at Detective Vance. His furious expression made me wince, but the pain in his eyes compelled me to deliver his sister's message.

"Um, Emily wants you to know something. 'Beneath the daffodils by my tree.' Does that mean anything to you?"

If possible, his complexion turned whiter, and rage quickly replaced the sadness in his eyes.

"I'm so sorry, Detective," I murmured. "I didn't mean to bring up painful memories."

Vance paced a few steps before stopping to look at me. His voice was a harsh whisper, barely contained fury lacing his words. He jabbed a shaking finger at me. "You think this is funny? Making up stories about my sister?"

His anger was palpable. I reared back in my chair but refused to back down. "I'm not making it up," I insisted. "I wish I was."

Red-faced and nearly vibrating with anger, Vance shook his head. "Get out," he spat suddenly, pointing toward the door, his composure cracking. "Get out now, but don't leave town. We're not done here. Not by a long shot."

I hurried out of the room, my heart pounding. I stepped into the harsh light of a beautiful Savannah spring, the encounter still pressing down on my shoulders. With a growing certainty, I knew that my life was about to change irrevocably.

8

PLAYING TOURIST

The afternoon sun streaming through the carriage house's French doors did little to dispel the dread that had settled deep in my bones after my encounter with Vance. Pacing, I paused every few steps, glancing toward the quiet street, half-expecting to see the detective's car pull up again.

Vance's imposing height, muscular build, and chiseled jawline had left a strong impression, intimidating and unyielding. The intensity in his steel-blue eyes was etched into my memory—cold, probing, and unwavering.

Unable to quiet my mind, I crossed the courtyard and entered the mansion, calling for Giles. I found him in his study, poring over an old book.

As I entered, I caught a glimpse of an illustration on the page—a snake curled into a circle, consuming its own tail.

Before I could fully register the image, Giles snapped the book shut and leaped to his feet.

"Lenox," Giles rushed across the room and grasped my hands, concern etched across his face. "What happened?"

"It was awful, Giles," I confessed, my voice trembling. "He—he thinks I might have something to do with Amelia's murder."

Giles's tone sharpened. "He said that?"

"Not directly, but the implication was there, especially after...I mentioned his sister." I shuddered, recalling Vance's fury at the mention of Emily. "He was so angry, Giles. I've never seen anything like it."

I stared at the intricately woven oriental carpet, tracing the elaborate pattern of scrolls and swirls with my eyes. Vance's reaction had been more than anger; it was a deep, painful wound I'd inadvertently reopened, and now I was questioning how I used my abilities. It was one thing to help a ghost find peace, but hurting the living in the process?

"I'm starting to wonder if using my gift is just...bringing more trouble than it's worth."

"Lenox," Giles said firmly, placing a comforting hand on my shoulder, "you can't let this shake your confidence. Your abilities are a gift, not just to you but to those spirits seeking peace. Perhaps take today off, go out, be a tourist for a day. Get to know the city a little better."

"But there's so much I still need to do," I protested, my voice thick with frustration. "The tours, the research—I can't just leave it all."

Giles's expression softened. "The work will still be here tomorrow, Lenox. And you'll handle it better with a clear mind. Trust me, a day away from all this might give you a new perspective."

Reluctantly, I agreed. "Maybe you're right. I'll try to clear my head."

The historic district was bustling, the lively sounds of street musicians blending with the rhythmic clip-clop of horse-drawn carriages. Refreshed from a delicious meal at La Paloma, I wandered through the cobblestone streets, soaking in the charm of Savannah's antique stores and boutiques.

After buying a new pair of jeans at a thrift store on Broughton Street, I stopped at a home furnishings shop and picked out a decorative pillow and throw blanket for the carriage house. As I walked down Bull Street, I remembered Clarke's Fine Art Gallery—the one I'd meant to visit after seeing that mesmerizing painting in the window.

With no real plans for the rest of the day, I grasped the brass handle of the gallery's wooden door and pushed it open, stepping inside with a contented sigh.

The gallery's interior was a haven of calm, the soft lighting perfectly highlighting the vibrant, thought-provoking paintings adorning the walls. The scent of polished wood mingled with faint traces of linseed oil, adding a timeless charm to the space. Gentle classical music hummed in the background, blending harmoniously with the quiet conversations of other patrons.

The painting I'd seen from the street—moonlight glistening on the water—was now hanging on the far wall. Its pull was magnetic, drawing me in until I stood transfixed before it. The delicate interplay of light and shadow on the river's surface stirred something deep within me, a sense of déjà vu I couldn't quite place.

"Beautiful, isn't it?"

Startled, I turned and found myself face-to-face with a man who seemed just as striking as the artwork. He was tall and impeccably dressed, his tailored suit exuding both elegance and ease. His green eyes sparkled with curiosity, and his smile was warm, revealing a dimple in his left cheek.

His presence was magnetic, his voice rich and smooth, with a timbre that seemed to resonate in the quiet gallery. My heart skipped a beat.

"It is," I replied, still somewhat dazed from the vivid memory the painting had stirred. "It feels familiar somehow."

He smiled, his dimple deepening. "That's the magic of art. It connects us to memories and emotions we didn't even know we had."

"I'm Julian Clarke," he introduced himself, extending his hand. "Welcome to my gallery."

"Lenox Grady," I said, shaking his hand. His grip was firm and warm, grounding me in the moment. "Your gallery is wonderful. I've been meaning to visit."

"I'm glad you did," Julian said, his gaze lingering on mine for a moment longer than expected. He stepped closer, and my pulse quickened, a warm flush creeping up my neck. The space between us hummed with palpable tension. I told myself to get a grip and focus on the art, not the charming man standing beside me.

"This is one of the finest pieces I've had the pleasure of displaying," he commented, his voice low and intimate. "The artist is local. He has a real knack for capturing the essence of Savannah's landscapes. This one, in particular, depicts the Moon River as seen from the Diamond Causeway."

The way Julian was looking at me made me a little breathless, but I managed to pull my gaze away from him and comment on the painting. "The way they've captured the moonlight on the water is mesmerizing. It feels so serene and timeless."

Julian's eyes lit up with pleasure at my response. "Exactly! It's all about the light, isn't it? The transition from day to night along the river can be enchanting. The artist really knows how to bring that to life."

I nodded, feeling a growing connection. "It almost feels like you're there, experiencing it firsthand. The details are incredible, right down to the reflections in the water."

"Yes," Julian agreed, stepping just a bit closer. "The reflections add so much depth. It's like the water is alive, shimmering under the moonlight. The artist's technique with light and shadow is truly remarkable."

I glanced at him, intrigued by his knowledge and passion. "Do you know the artist personally? It seems like you have a deep appreciation for their work."

He smiled, a hint of mystery in his eyes. "I do. We've worked together for several years now. Each piece he creates is a new discovery, a new exploration of Savannah's beauty. It's fascinating to see his growth and evolution as an artist."

"I can imagine," I replied, my heart skipping a beat at the intensity in his gaze. "It must be wonderful to be surrounded by such creativity every day."

"It is," Julian said softly. "Art has a way of connecting people, of telling stories that words often can't capture. It's why

I love what I do. And it's always a pleasure to meet some-one who appreciates it as much as I do."

I smiled, feeling a warm flush creeping up my neck. "I'm drawn to art. There's something magical about the way it can evoke emotions and memories."

Julian nodded, his expression thoughtful. "Absolutely. Art can transport us to different times and places, making us feel things we didn't know we could feel. It's a powerful medium."

His passion and the sincerity in his voice captivated me. "You speak about it with such reverence. It's inspiring."

He held my gaze, the connection between us growing stronger. "Thank you, Lenox. It means a lot to hear that. If you like this, there are a few more pieces by the same artist around the gallery. Maybe you'd like a tour? I'd love to show you more of our collection."

My pulse quickened at the prospect of spending more time with him. "I'd love that, thank you!"

As we walked through the gallery, Julian pointed out var-ious artworks, each with a story that seemed to bring the pieces to life. His knowledge was impressive, and his passion for art infectious.

"You have an eye for detail," he noted, watching me as I studied a particularly striking portrait.

"Thank you," I laughed softly, brushing a strand of hair from my face. "I guess I just get lost in the beauty of it all. It's like stepping into another world."

"Well"—his tone was playful, his gaze intent—"consider yourself officially invited to step into my world anytime."

Caught off guard by his forwardness, I blushed. His wide grin said he'd noticed, but gentleman that he was, he didn't comment. Instead, he smoothly changed the subject.

"Tonight is our monthly amateur art event. A local art teacher instructs on basic techniques, and then we all settle at our easels with a glass or three of wine and paint our hearts out." His eyes gleamed as he looked down at me, his voice low and intimate. "Would you join me?"

The invitation was unexpected, but the thought of spending more time with Julian was too enticing to pass up. "I'd love to," I agreed, smiling.

His smile could have lit the room. "Wonderful! Tonight at seven, shall I pick you up?"

I shook my head, a little flustered by his intensity. "No need to trouble yourself, I just live across the square."

He picked up my hand, his thumb rubbing lazy circles over my palm. "No trouble at all, I assure you."

My fingers trembled, and I was sure he noticed my fluttering pulse. I gently extracted my hand and smiled. "Well, I appreciate the offer, but I can manage."

I couldn't deny my attraction to him but letting him know where I lived didn't seem like the wisest decision just yet. I'd attend his event, but before I spent any time alone with him, I wanted to see what Giles knew about him.

"All right then," Julian said, his voice smooth, "but I hope you won't change your mind." He walked me to the door.

As I stepped outside, Julian took my hand again and raised it to his lips. "I've enjoyed our time this afternoon, Lenox, and hope you'll let me get to know you better."

Butterflies fluttered in my stomach, and my hand burned like he'd branded me. Drawing a shaky breath, I smiled. "I—I'd like to get to know you better, too."

His lips twisted into a sexy smile. "Until tonight then..."

On cloud nine, I almost floated home. Tonight, I decided, would be the start of something new—both in my life and in my heart.

9
THE ART OF ROMANCE

The gallery buzzed with conversation and the soft clinking of wine glasses. Julian's art party was in full swing, causing a blend of excitement and nerves to bubble inside me. I hadn't been in this world of art and social gatherings for long, and it still overwhelmed me at times.

"Lenox, I'd like you to meet Victor," Julian said, guiding me through the crowd with a hand lightly placed on the small of my back. His touch lingered longer than necessary, sending a brief shiver up my spine. "He's a talented artist and teaches at the local college."

Victor, tall with dark hair and an intense gaze, greeted me with a smile that softened the sharpness in his eyes. "Nice to meet you, Lenox. I've heard great things."

"Nice to meet you too," I said, feeling the weight of his scrutiny.

"Excited to put some paint on canvas?"

I laughed nervously. "Well, not sure it'll be good, but I'm game."

Victor chuckled. "That's the spirit."

Victor was soon pulled away by another guest, leaving Julian and me alone. As we moved through the gallery, Julian introduced me to a whirlwind of people. I was struck by how easily he commanded attention—he was charming, gracious, and everyone seemed drawn to him. Several women cast me envious glances, their eyes lingering on him with more than admiration for his art.

Julian led me to a pristine easel near the still life Victor had set up. "Here we are," he said, his voice warm. "Best spot in the house." He took my hand, brushing a kiss across my palm. "Enjoy yourself. I'll check in on you later."

After he left, I took in the still life: a brass vase with magnolia blossoms, an earthenware jug, and a doll in a blue dress. It was a scene I could lose myself in, but my focus was shaky. As

I picked up the brush, I could still feel the phantom warmth of Julian's kiss on my skin. It made me feel...claimed.

Shaking the thought, I began blocking in the background with soft oranges and yellows. Painting felt natural, as if my hand knew exactly what to do. The room around me blurred as I lost myself in the rhythm, my brush sweeping across the canvas.

Suddenly, the world around me seemed to fade.

Sunlight streamed through a bank of windows, casting light on the scattered easels, paint-splattered floor, and shelves filled with art supplies. The room was suffused with a golden glow, the light dancing off glass jars and metal tools lined up on shelves. The scent of paint and turpentine mingled with the sweet perfume of roses in a vase perched on the windowsill.

Sitting on an easel near the windows was a painting of a forest. The full moon hung low over the ocean, casting tall pines in shadow. I dipped my brush into a dark green puddle on my palette, picking up a bit of black before adding another layer of trees.

To the right of the forest was a clearing that led to the ocean. A blazing bonfire on the edge of the beach turned the sand to liquid gold. I studied the fire, then used charcoal gray to create the silhouette of a woman.

My breath caught in my throat. The vision was so vivid, so real. My hand moved instinctively, as if this scene was one I had painted before. But that was impossible. Wasn't it?

"Lenox? Lenox…" Julian's voice broke through my concentration, yanking me back to the present. He waved a hand in front of my face, making me jump.

Julian smirked, his eyes searching mine with an intensity that made my heart stutter. "You were in your own world there. I called your name a few times."

I forced a smile. "Sorry, I got lost in the painting."

Victor leaned in to study my work. "And what a piece it is. I love the detail you added to the doll's dress. The Ouroboros is a nice touch."

I blinked at the canvas, surprised to see a golden snake coiled around the doll's dress, its head devouring its tail. I didn't remember painting it.

Julian's expression sharpened, though his smile stayed in place. "Interesting choice," he murmured, his voice smooth. "The Ouroboros is a powerful symbol. Sometimes, our subconscious knows things we don't."

Victor's smile widened as he leaned in farther, his gaze lingering on the Ouroboros. "You've got an incredible eye for detail, Lenox," he said, his voice smooth but with an undertone I couldn't quite place. "The Ouroboros...you chose a powerful symbol. One that's been associated with immortality and cycles of creation."

My heart skipped a beat. The Ouroboros had appeared before—in my dreams, and again when I walked through the city. What was it trying to tell me? Why did it feel like it belonged, as if I'd always known it?

I swallowed to clear my suddenly dry throat. "I...I didn't really think about it," I replied, trying to shake off the feeling. "It just...happened."

Victor's eyes darkened for a fraction of a second before his smile returned. "Sometimes the best art comes from deep within, from places we don't fully understand." His voice was low, almost conspiratorial. "I've always believed that true talent has a power of its own—something alive, something more."

A prickle of discomfort settled on my skin. There was something unsettling in the way he spoke, as if he saw more in the painting than I had intended.

Julian's voice cut through the tension, light and easy. "Victor's always had a way of seeing deeper into art than most," he said, though his tone wasn't as relaxed as usual. I caught the briefest flicker of something unreadable in his eyes before he smiled at me.

Victor's gaze remained on the Ouroboros, almost too focused. He straightened, finally tearing his eyes away from the painting. "You've got considerable talent, Lenox," he said, the smoothness of his voice returning. "Have you thought about taking classes? I teach a summer course for beginners at the college. You don't need to be enrolled, and it's affordable."

Caught off guard by his enthusiasm, I shifted my gaze back to the painting. "Oh, I don't know. I've never really taken lessons before."

"You should think about it," Julian added, his hand sliding onto my shoulder, squeezing gently. "You have real potential. And it would give you more time to explore your talent."

I blushed, ducking my head slightly. "Thanks. I'll think about it."

Maybe I would. Painting had been relaxing, and something about the act of creating stirred a deeper sense of familiarity. Could taking classes unlock more than just skill? The thought tugged at me, even as the conversation moved on.

The rest of the evening passed in a blur of conversations and laughter as everyone finished their paintings. Conscious of the time, I'd rushed to finish and that left me a little dissatisfied with the project. I laughed to myself, thinking I definitely had the temperament to be an artist.

As the party wound down, Julian found me again, his expression warm but laced with something I couldn't quite name. "I'll walk you home," he offered, stepping closer. His words weren't pushy, but there was a weight behind them.

I hesitated, the memory of my earlier caution flickering. But Giles had assured me Julian was well-respected in the community, and his warmth tonight felt genuine, not threatening. I nodded, the weight of my earlier apprehension lifting.

"Sure," I said, my voice lighter this time. "I'd appreciate that."

As we walked through the quiet streets of Savannah, the air between us was charged, humming with unspoken energy. Julian's hand brushed mine occasionally, the brief contact sending a strange thrill through me. I couldn't ignore the magnetic pull that had formed between us, even though a voice in the back of my mind whispered caution.

When we reached my door, Julian paused, turning to face me. The soft glow of the streetlamp cast his features in shadow, but I could feel the weight of his gaze.

"I had a wonderful time tonight," he said, his voice low, intimate. His hand reached up to tuck a stray lock of hair behind my ear, his touch lingering longer than it should.

I nodded, my heart racing. "Me too."

Julian stepped closer, our breaths mingling as he leaned in, his lips inches from mine. The moment stretched, heavy with anticipation.

"You're incredible, Lenox," he murmured, his voice barely above a whisper. "I've wanted to do this all night."

The world around us faded, leaving only the two of us in the circle of light. His hand cupped my cheek, warm and steady, but before our lips could meet—

"We need to talk."

10

A WORLD REVEALED

Julian and I stood frozen in the doorway, the romantic tension between us shattered by Detective Vance's sudden arrival. His serious expression tightened the atmosphere, dissolving any remnants of the intimate moment we had shared.

"Detective Vance," I said, trying to steady my voice. "What's this about?"

Julian's hand slipped away from mine as he took a cautious step back, his eyes flicking between Vance and me. The shift from near-kiss to confrontation was jarring, leaving an uneasy silence in its wake.

Vance stepped forward, his gaze never wavering. "We need to talk," he said again, his tone brooking no delay. "It's urgent."

I glanced at Julian, who looked both curious and concerned. Nodding, I fumbled with my keys and unlocked the door to my apartment. "Come in," I said, pushing the door open and stepping aside. Vance walked in, leaving Julian and me standing on the porch.

Julian hesitated, his gaze flickering between me and the open door Vance had walked through. I could tell he had questions and braced myself to tell a little white lie, but after holding my gaze for a long second, he reached into his pocket and pulled out a business card.

"Call me when you're free," he said softly, pressing the card into my hand. He lifted my hand to his lips, brushing a gentle kiss across my knuckles. "I had a wonderful evening. Take care."

As his lips touched my hand, a warm shiver ran through me, momentarily overshadowing the anxiety brought by Vance's interruption. "Thank you, Julian," I whispered, appreciating his tact and touched by his kindness despite the abrupt end to our evening.

He gave me a reassuring smile before stepping back. "Good night, Lenox." With a final glance, he turned and walked away, his footsteps echoing softly in the night.

I watched Julian disappear into the shadows, my heart caught in a confusing whirl of emotions. The disappointment of our interrupted kiss mingled with a lingering warmth from his touch, leaving me yearning for more.

Yet, the reality of Vance's presence grounded me, reminding me of the seriousness of the situation at hand. Taking a deep breath, I turned back toward the apartment and stepped inside, closing the door behind me. The romantic tension had shifted into something else, charged with urgency and unanswered questions.

Vance was waiting patiently, his expression still serious. "Alright, Detective," I said, trying to steady my racing thoughts. "What's so urgent?"

Vance glanced around the room briefly before his eyes settled back on me. "I went to my childhood home today," he began, his voice tinged with unresolved memories. "There's a tree by the creek, a favorite place for kids to play. It had a swing that we'd use to sail out over the water and jump in."

I nodded, sensing this was leading somewhere important but unsure where.

"Emily and I used to spend hours there," Vance continued, his voice softening with the recollection. "It was her favorite spot. She loved that tree."

An image of Emily's smiling face flashed in my mind, making my heart ache. She'd been so young, so full of life and promise. "Is that why Emily told me about that place?" I asked.

Vance's eyes darkened with both sorrow and determination. "The morning she went missing…" His voice cracked. He swallowed hard before continuing. "She begged me to come out and play, but I'd just made the junior varsity baseball team and wanted to practice. I told her, 'Take a hike, kid.'"

The words ended on a sob, and my instinct was to wrap the big man in a hug and offer comfort, but Vance turned away, swiping at his eyes as he stared out the French doors. His shoulders shook a few times and then he drew a deep breath and turned back toward me.

"Sorry," he sniffed. "I just…"

This time I gave rein to my instincts and reached out, squeezing his shoulder. "It's all right, it's a horrible tragedy and I'm so sorry I brought it up."

His blue eyes burned with intensity as he shook his head. "Don't be. I...I was angry when you first told me but when I went to that tree, I remembered what you said Emily told you. 'Beneath the daffodils by my tree.' So I dug around and found this."

He pulled a small, rusty metal box from his bag and handed it to me. "It was buried near the base of the tree, just where Emily said it would be."

I opened the box with trembling hands. Inside were small trinkets: a beautiful diamond pendant on a gold chain, a few notes written in childish handwriting, a small toy, and a diary. Tears welled up in my eyes as I looked through the keepsakes, each one a testament to Emily's short but precious life.

"Emily's spirit must have guided you to find this," I whispered, touched by the tangible connection to her.

"I don't know how to explain this," Vance said, running a hand through his hair. "Part of me still thinks I'm losing it, but...this box was right where Emily said it would be."

He swallowed, his voice tight with disbelief. "I can't ignore that."

I nodded, letting him process what he was saying. "You believe me now?"

He hesitated, his brow furrowing. "I believe *something's* happening. It's hard to wrap my head around, but Emily.. .she's reaching out to us. And if what you're saying is true, I need your help to find out what happened to her."

I nodded slowly. "I'll try to get more information from her," I promised, my voice steady despite the emotions swirling inside me. "But Derek, this isn't an exact science. I don't always know how it's going to work."

"I get it," he said, his voice softer now. "But I don't know where else to turn. If she's really talking to you... I'll take whatever help I can get."

Vance's shoulders relaxed slightly, a hint of hope in his eyes. "Thank you, Lenox. This means a lot to me."

I met his gaze, sensing the shift in him. But I wasn't sure if he was all the way there yet. "Do you believe me? About Amelia?"

He paused, his jaw tightening as he weighed his words. "Look, I believe you're not making this up. Finding that box..." He sighed, rubbing the back of his neck. "It changed things for me. But Amelia's case...that's different." He took a deep breath, meeting my eyes with quiet determination. "I'll need more to go on before I fully believe. But I'm willing to try."

I cleared my throat. "So, you want me to try and contact Emily again?" He nodded, and I added. "And Amelia? Do you want help finding her killer?"

He winced. "I do, if you're willing. But it'll have to be unofficial. We use consultants sometimes, but I'd be laughed out of the department if I asked to hire a psychic."

I laughed. "Believe me, I understand completely. Not too long ago, I was pretty sure either I or Giles was crazy, but then Amelia spoke to me, and I couldn't ignore what was happening any longer."

Vance gave a small, appreciative smile, but his eyes held a determination that matched my own. He looked around my cozy living room and clapped his hands.

"So, what do you need to contact Amelia? Do you hold a séance or...?"

I chuckled. "No, at least I never have before." I swallowed hard, remembering how it ended the night Giles took me to deliberately make contact with a spirit. "Um, I've never deliberately contacted a ghost."

Vance's eyebrows shot up, and he frowned. "Then, how?"

I shrugged. "Well, they just sort of find me. I really don't know much beyond the fact that I can see and talk to the dead."

I glanced at the clock sitting on the mantel. It was five minutes before midnight. The ghost tours started at ten and lasted about an hour and a half, which meant Giles should be on his way home.

"I'd like to talk things over with my boss. Giles is the one that knows about all of this spooky stuff."

Vance chuckled. "Okay." He yawned, causing a sympathetic response in me.

I laughed and crossed to the door. "It's getting late. Why don't we start in the morning? We can plan our approach and make sure we're prepared."

Vance nodded and followed me. "That sounds good. Where do you think we should begin?"

I hesitated, thinking it over. "We should start where I first saw Amelia's ghost, the Quill and Brew coffee shop. But we can't contact her in the middle of a busy café, so I don't know..."

Vance frowned. "Does the location matter? Can't you do it here?"

"It's usually easier for the ghost if they're in a familiar place," I explained. "It helps them connect better."

Vance's eyes lit up with a sudden idea. "I can get access to Amelia's apartment. Would that work?"

"Yes, that's perfect," I said, feeling a surge of hope.

"Then it's settled. Meet me at the Quill and Brew tomorrow morning at ten."

I frowned, confused. "The Quill? But there'll be too many people for me to try and contact Amelia."

Vance laughed. "I heard you. But we're not going into the coffee shop. Amelia lived in an apartment above it."

"Oh, right. I forgot." I grimaced at the thought of visiting a crime scene, but if I wanted to help Vance, it couldn't be helped. "Okay, Giles and I'll be there."

After closing the door, I leaned against it, my mind racing. Tomorrow, I would be stepping further into the unknown, guided by ghosts and the desperate need for answers.

II

VIOLENT VISIONS

Mr. Langford, the owner of the building housing both the Quill and Brew and Amelia Walsh's former apartment, led Vance, Giles, and me up a set of highly polished, cherry wood steps. As we ascended, he kept a running commentary on the trials and tribulations of running a coffee shop and being a landlord.

"Lucky timing, detective." He unlocked the door to apartment one and stepped aside. "New tenants move in next Friday, though I doubt they'll stay long."

Sensing Vance's annoyance with the garrulous man, I engaged him in conversation while Vance and Giles went over the plans for contacting Amelia.

"Why don't you expect your new tenant to live here long, Mr. Langford?"

He scoffed. "Rented this unit twice since Amelia was killed, God rest her soul, and both broke their lease within six months."

My eyes widened. "Wouldn't that mean they forfeited their deposit?"

He nodded. "Yep, only reason I wasn't too angry about it." He smirked. "What do they say about fools and their money?"

Curiosity piqued, I pressed further. "Why did they leave so quickly?"

He rolled his eyes. "Both tenants claimed the place was haunted. Said they saw and heard things they couldn't explain."

From the corner of my eye, I saw Giles glance over. Our gazes met, and he raised an eyebrow before nodding toward the landlord. Taking the hint, I feigned surprise.

"Haunted? Really? Did you ever notice anything unusual while Amelia lived here?"

He rolled his eyes and shook his head. "No, darn fools were just letting their imaginations run wild because they knew Amelia died here." He huffed. "Believe me, if there was any weird stuff happening in that apartment, Amelia would have noticed. She worked from home and was here pretty much all day and night."

Derek had introduced Giles and me as consultants looking into a cold case, which was fortunate, considering Mr. Langford was clearly skeptical about ghosts. My lips twitched, but I suppressed the urge to grin. If he only knew the real reason we'd asked to see Amelia's apartment!

"So, Amelia worked from home. What did she do for a living?"

Mr. Langford chuckled. "She wrote for some paranormal magazine or some such nonsense. Always had her nose in a book or tapping away on her laptop."

Giles, who had been pretending to examine the room, turned his full attention to Mr. Langford. "Paranormal magazine, you say? Did she ever mention what kind of things she wrote about?"

The landlord shrugged. "Ghosts, spirits, the occult. Her apartment was filled with books and papers on the subject. When we cleaned out the place, we found salt around the window sills and other things that are supposed to protect against the occult."

Giles and Vance exchanged a look, clearly recognizing the significance of this. It was more than just an interesting detail—it could be a crucial piece of the puzzle.

"So she was trying to protect herself from something," Giles mused, scanning the room with renewed interest.

Mr. Langford nodded. "Seems so. Whatever it was, looks like she might've had good reason to be cautious."

A shiver crept through me. "Well, let's hope we can find out exactly what that was."

Once Mr. Langford left, I locked the door and joined Vance and Giles in the empty living room. The room was elegant yet lifeless, its former warmth replaced by a sterile stillness. The high ceilings and antique light fixtures contrasted with the hollow silence.

Giles was in the middle of sprinkling salt in a circular pattern on the floor, murmuring a prayer under his breath. When he finished, he straightened and motioned me over.

"You'll have to finish the rest, Lenox. Do you remember how to complete the protection ritual?"

I nodded, mentally reviewing Giles's instructions. White candles, placed at the cardinal points, represented purity and protection. I anointed them with oil as Giles had taught me, ensuring we were shielded from any malevolent forces.

Once I placed the last candle, I picked up a book of matches, ready to light them. Vance and Giles stepped inside the circle, and I struck the first match, bringing the flame to the northern candle's wick. As the flame flickered to life, I began reciting the incantation Giles had drilled into me:

"Spirits of protection, hear my call,

Guard this circle, guard us all.

With light and salt, we seal this space,

Keep us safe in your embrace.

By fire and root, by herb and oil,

Protect us from harm, guard our toil."

I continued moving clockwise, lighting each candle and repeating the chant. With each flame, the room seemed to change. The air grew warmer, and the faint scent of rosemary filled the space, as though the very atmosphere was alive, reacting to the ritual.

The final candle was burning brightly when Giles handed me a small purple candle. "Sit in the center and light this one. It'll help draw Amelia's spirit and give her a focal point."

I nodded, taking the candle and sitting cross-legged in the middle of the circle. I closed my eyes, taking several deep breaths as Giles's voice guided me into a meditative state. His words were soft and steady, like a calming rhythm in the back of my mind.

"Breathe, Lenox. Let everything go. Focus only on Amelia. Picture her here with you."

Focusing on the rise and fall of my chest, I allowed the image of Amelia's red hair and smiling face to solidify in my mind. "Amelia? I'm Lenox. You told me the angels sang you to sleep. I'm here to help."

For a moment, there was nothing. But then, the air around me shifted, cold and sharp. Goosebumps prickled my arms, and I heard a faint whisper: "Weak...can't..."

I swallowed hard, struggling to understand. "Amelia, are you saying you're too weak?"

Another gust of cold air swirled around me.

I frowned, trying to think. There had to be a way to give her more energy. Giles had once mentioned that spirits could sometimes draw energy from their surroundings, even draining electronics. Maybe I could offer her my phone's battery?

A gentle thrum from the tourmaline stone around my neck made me pause. The stone's energy pulsed through me like a current. Could Amelia draw energy from it, from me?

I extended my hand, speaking softly. "Amelia, take my hand. Use me to get stronger."

A misty form appeared before me, and I felt a zap of energy as it wrapped around my hand. Behind me, Giles gasped, but I shook my head. "I'm fine, Giles. She just needs a little boost..."

Then, everything went black.

When I opened my eyes, I was standing in Amelia's apartment—but it was no longer empty. The room was filled with furniture, the warmth of a life once lived evident in every detail. Amelia sat at a desk, her back to me, typing away on her laptop.

"Amelia!" I called, but she didn't respond. I frowned, moving closer. Was this a memory?

The floor creaked, and Amelia stiffened. A shadow moved in the corner of the room, rushing toward her. She turned, just as a figure in a black cloak lunged at her with a silver dagger. The blade plunged into her chest, and Amelia let out a scream that echoed in my mind.

The killer's voice rasped, "Pale moon, deliver..." and the speaker on Amelia's desk began playing "Moon River" in haunting, lilting tones.

I wanted to scream, to stop it, but I was frozen. I watched in horror as Amelia's life drained away, her body crumpling to the floor. The killer bent down, cutting a lock of her hair and sprinkling something over her body.

As the vision shattered, I was back in the apartment with Giles and Vance, my body trembling from the shock of what I had just witnessed.

"Lenox?" Giles was kneeling beside me, his voice full of concern. "What happened? What did you see?"

I took a shaky breath. "I...I saw her murder...the killer...the dagger..." My voice faltered as the memory replayed in vivid detail.

Vance stepped closer, his expression grim. "Did you see their face?"

I shook my head, still dazed. "No. They were wearing a black cloak. I couldn't tell if it was a man or a woman. But they...they said something. 'Pale moon, deliver.' And then...then they cut a lock of her hair."

Giles and Vance exchanged a troubled look.

"The dagger," Giles said quietly. "What did it look like?"

I closed my eyes, focusing on the image of the blade. "It was silver, ornate...with strange symbols carved into it."

I quickly sketched the dagger from memory, my hand trembling as I handed the drawing to Giles.

His face paled as he looked at it. "I've seen this before," he murmured.

"What does it mean?" I asked.

"I'm not sure yet," Giles replied, his voice grim. "But I'll need to consult with some...colleagues."

Derek raised an eyebrow. "Colleagues? Are you saying there's a community of, what, supernatural experts?"

Giles chuckled. "Indeed, Detective. Savannah is full of surprises. And once the sun goes down, you'll get to meet them."

12

INTO THE TWILIGHT

Clinging to the metal handrail, I gingerly followed Derek and Giles down the stone stairs leading to the lower level of Factor's Walk. My limbs dragged, a dull ache pulsing through my head—a lingering reminder of the energy I had given Amelia earlier. Even after the nap Giles had suggested, the bone-deep fatigue clung to me, refusing to let go.

We reached the bottom of the steep staircase, but instead of continuing down the ramp that led to River Street, Giles turned right into an alley so dark it seemed to swallow the light. The cobblestones were uneven and slick, forcing me to concentrate on each step.

"I thought we were heading to a bar. They're all on River Street," Derek said, his voice echoing slightly.

"Twilight Tavern has a more discreet entrance," Giles replied. "It's safer this way."

As we ventured deeper into the alley, the sounds of River Street faded, replaced by the distant hum of the city. Through gaps in the buildings, I caught glimpses of the Savannah River, its briny scent mingling with the dampness of the alley. The cold night air did little to alleviate my fatigue. Each step seemed to sap what little energy I had left, a constant reminder of the cost of using my abilities.

Giles paused at the entrance to a dark room cut into the side of the bluff, waiting for me to catch up. I forced my legs to increase pace, but it cost me; I was panting and shaky when I reached them.

"Lenox, did you take my advice and rest this afternoon?" Giles frowned.

"Yes, though I don't think it did any good," I admitted.

He pursed his lips. "This new ability comes with consequences. We'll need to discuss the safest ways of sharing or directing your energy before you attempt such a thing again." By his expression and tone, I knew he was telling me not to do it again.

"Believe me, if I'd known the result was feeling like this, I wouldn't have attempted it."

Giles smiled. "We'll talk about this more later. For now, we'll focus on getting information about that dagger." He tipped his head, indicating we should follow him.

Instead of continuing up the alley, Giles turned and walked through a brick archway.

"Uh, Giles? What is this place?" I asked.

"This is one of the Clusky Embankment Stores, locally known as the Clusky tombs. They were originally extra storage for the ports."

"Interesting. But I thought we were going to a tavern. This room is empty," I noted, feeling a bit spooked by the vaulted ceilings and damp brick walls that gave the space an unsettling vibe.

Giles led us to a seemingly solid wall at the end of the tomb. "Where's the tavern? This is a dead end."

Giles smiled cryptically and fished a medallion from his waistcoat pocket. He waved it at a brick on the wall. The brick shimmered, the surface rippling like water, and then it vanished, revealing another alley beyond.

Blinking in surprise, I started to ask how he'd done it when Giles stepped aside, gesturing for us to proceed.

"After you," he said with a flourish.

Eyes wide, I glanced at Derek before stepping through, stifling a laugh when he started humming the Twilight Zone theme as he followed me. We'd only taken a few steps when a flash of light illuminated the cobblestones. I turned in time to see the archway morph back into a brick wall.

"Giles!" I pointed at the wall. "What was that?"

"There are more things on heaven and earth, my dear Lenox..." He chuckled and waved for us to follow. "Come, there is no time to lose."

The alley twisted and turned before we reached an ancient oak door, its surface etched with intricate runes that seemed to shimmer in the dim light. Set into a wall of moss-covered stone, the door looked as if it had always been there, waiting.

A sign hanging above it revealed we'd found the Twilight Tavern. I couldn't figure out how the tavern existed or how the path led to it. The tombs were built into the bluff behind River Street—were we now beneath them?

Nothing made sense, and my exhausted brain said don't even try. Shaking my head, I glanced at Derek. He shrugged and held his hand out for me to precede him.

We followed Giles through the door, stopping on the threshold while our eyes adjusted to the dim lighting. The inside of the Twilight Tavern was similar to the tomb hiding its entrance. A warm, golden light glowed from lanterns hung on the weathered brick walls, casting eerie shadows.

Round tables with red upholstered chairs, heart pine floors, and a small stage took up one-half of the room, with a long bar running along the back wall. A pool table and a couple of video games occupied the other end.

Derek leaned over and whispered in my ear. "Looks like any other bar on River Street. I thought this was some supernatural hangout."

"Yeah, except for that." I pointed to the bar. A white trellis was suspended from the ceiling, and ivy twined among the slats. Two cabbage palms stood guard at either end.

Once my eyes fully adjusted, I looked around and gasped. "Look," I nodded toward a stage set against the back wall. "Is that...but how?"

"It's a live oak! The stage is literally the lower limb of that tree!" Derek's mouth dropped open.

"I don't understand... How can a huge tree be growing in here? There are no windows, no grow lights, and the ceiling..." Amazed, I met Derek's eyes. "This is nuts!"

"We aren't in Kansas anymore, that's for sure." He gulped and nodded.

I was about to make a smart remark when Giles started weaving his way around the tables, heading to the bar. The path he took gave me an up-close view of the other patrons, and it was all I could do not to stare.

Two women with long silver hair and pointed ears were conversing with a man covered in shiny green scales. At another table, a tiny woman with iridescent skin and fluttering wings flirted with a—a person covered in black fur.

Everywhere I looked, there were strange beings, and I wondered how they were living among us. Savannah was a tolerant city, but encountering these people would start a riot!

I glanced at Derek and saw he was just as stupefied. "These people are living around us? How can they hide in plain sight?" he murmured.

"Was thinking the same thing. Maybe disguises?"

He let out a short laugh. "Must own stock in makeup!"

Giles, who had been weaving his way around the tables with purpose, finally reached the bar. He turned and beckoned us over. "Come on, you two."

We hurried to join him, not wanting to be left behind in this bewildering place. As we approached the bar, I gasped. Giles was shaking hands with the man I'd seen at Selena's shop!

A flutter of excitement stirred in my chest as his gaze briefly swung toward me. What was it about the man that made my pulse quicken? Yes, he was attractive, but so was Julian and many other men.

There was something about him and the way he looked at me. When his vivid blue eyes met mine, it was like he could see all the way to my soul, and whatever he saw amused him.

If pressed, I wouldn't be able to fully explain, but his gaze held a note of challenge, as if he were testing me. The oddest thing was, I got the impression he was hoping I'd pass.

The smirk on his face seemed to be perpetual and not directed specifically at me. His gaze swung to me, and he winked, making me flush and look away.

"Lenox, Derek, this is Reed. Reed, these are my companions," Giles said, clearing his throat.

Reed smiled. "A pleasure to meet you both." His eyes sparkled with humor as he took my hand. "We meet again, Little Spark."

My heart skipped a beat as his low, melodic tone rolled over me and the nickname was almost affectionate. It was like he knew some inside joke I wasn't privy to. I bit my lip and studied him from beneath my lashes. This man was dangerous. Whether to my safety or emotions was still to be determined.

I shook off my fascination with Reed as Giles continued. "Reed is a fae. He started the Twilight Tavern as a sanctuary for supernatural beings passing through our realm."

Realm? I blinked and looked at Giles. His statement implied there were others. I started to ask, but Derek chuckled and waved a hand at the room. "That explains the tree and flowers. Magic, right?"

Reed quirked a brow and smiled. "Perhaps." He looked at Giles. "Now, what brings you to the Twilight Tavern?"

Giles pulled out my drawing and handed it to Reed. "Lenox saw this dagger. We need to know if you recognize it."

The humor fell from his face as he studied my drawing. "This is a dagger used in dark magic," he said slowly, running his finger along the symbols decorating the hilt. "Someone is swimming in a very deep, dark pool." His intense gaze met mine. "Where did you see this, Little Spark?"

A shiver ran down my spine as Reed's words sank in. *Dark magic.* I wasn't sure what that entailed exactly, but it felt like a warning meant just for me. As if this dagger—and the power it held—wasn't done with me yet.

I managed to explain the circumstances as best as I could, recounting how I had contacted the ghost of Amelia Walsh and was shown how someone in a black cloak had stabbed her with the dagger. Reed listened intently, his brow furrowing as he processed the information.

Before he could respond, a tall, dark-haired man standing to the side of us turned and cleared his throat. "Excuse me, but did you say Amelia Walsh?" His voice was smooth and curious.

"Yes, Dante. Why do you ask?" Giles turned to him.

Dante's eyes shifted to me. "Someone by that name came in a few months ago asking questions. What did she look like?"

I described Amelia's long red hair and pretty brown eyes.

Dante nodded slowly. "Yes, that's her," he confirmed. "She was in here asking about the thefts of bodies from mortuaries."

"Thefts of—Was she a regular here?" Giles raised an eyebrow.

Dante shook his head. "No, and I was curious how she got hold of a medallion and even knew about the tavern since she was human."

My mind raced over what he'd said. "What kind of questions was she asking?"

"She wanted to know if anyone had heard about the recent body thefts and if there was a connection to any dark rituals," Dante explained. "It sounded like she was onto something, but she didn't share much detail."

So Amelia had been investigating, and thefts of bodies no less! Could that have been what got her killed? It seemed probable, especially since the killer had taken a notebook and her laptop.

The scene in Amelia's living room flashed before my eyes, making me shudder. I took a deep breath, trying to process everything. Amelia's death wasn't just a random act of violence; it was targeted. Someone wanted to silence her. The thought made my stomach churn.

If Amelia had been on the trail of something significant, then whoever killed her might still be out there, looking to cover their tracks. And Reed had said the dagger was used in dark magic. I wasn't sure what that entailed, but it sounded bad. If the killer was using magic, it was possible they knew we'd contacted Amelia. Had we just made ourselves a target?

The weight of it all pressed down on me, and a wave of dizziness washed over me. My vision blurred, and I stumbled, barely catching myself on the edge of the bar.

"Lenox!" Derek exclaimed, reaching out to steady me.

I tried to wave him off, but my legs felt like jelly. "I'm fine," I muttered, though it was clear to everyone that I wasn't.

"You don't look fine," Dante said softly, his concerned gaze fixed on me. "What happened?"

Giles stepped in, his tone serious. "Lenox allowed a spirit to feed off her energy earlier."

Dante's eyes widened slightly, then softened with understanding. "You gave your energy to a spirit?" he asked, his voice filled with both admiration and concern.

I nodded weakly. "Amelia...she needed help. I...I didn't even know such a thing was possible." I gave a shaky laugh. "So I also didn't know it would leave me like this."

Dante reached into his coat pocket and pulled out a small vial filled with a shimmering violet liquid. "Here, drink this. It should help restore some of your energy."

I looked at Giles, who nodded encouragement. With a shaky hand, I took the vial, hesitating for a moment before drinking its contents. My eyes widened as warmth flowed through me. A few seconds after it hit my stomach a bit of the fatigue lift.

"There you go. That should keep you on your feet for a while longer," Dante smiled reassuringly.

"Thank you," I said, genuinely grateful. "What was that?"

"Anytime. It's the least I can do for someone who's helped a spirit in need." He glanced at Reed, and something seemed to pass between the two.

After a second, Reed shrugged and looked at me. I frowned, trying to decipher the undercurrent, but when Dante started talking, I lost focus.

"The vial contained stores of emotional energy that I've harvested. As a psychic vampire, I feed on emotions rather than blood. I keep some of the harvested energy for emergencies like this. It's a temporary fix, but it should keep you going for a while."

Dante's expression grew more serious. "But Lenox, you need to be careful with giving your energy like that. It's admirable, but it can be very dangerous. You could deplete yourself to the point of no return. Always ensure you have a way to replenish what you give away."

Giles nodded in agreement. "There are safety precautions you must learn before attempting such a thing again."

"Believe me, I've learned my lesson!"

"Directing energy is a rare and valuable ability but you need to understand it in order to take care of yourself." Dante smiled reassuringly.

Giles thanked Reed and Dante, and we all turned to leave. As we made our way back through the tavern, a sense of unease settled over me. The supernatural beings around us were fascinating, but the realization that we were dealing with something powerful and potentially deadly lingered in my thoughts.

Outside, the cool night air hit me, and I shivered, partly from the cold and partly from the fear of what lay ahead. Derek placed a reassuring hand on my shoulder, and I gave him a grateful smile.

"We'll figure this out," he said confidently. "Together."

I nodded, amazement bubbling up inside me. Less than forty-eight hours ago, he'd been ready to lock me up for Amelia's murder, or at least for knowing too much about it.

Now, he not only believed in my ability to speak with ghosts, but he was also actively working with me to solve Amelia's murder. It was a reminder that there was always hope, even in the darkest of times.

Giles stopped just outside the secret entrance and turned to us, his expression serious. "If this is dark magic at work, there is no time to lose."

"Lenox." He looked at me. "Amelia was asking questions about a string of body thefts from mortuaries. We need background on those thefts. There must be some news reports on the incidents. Find those articles, and we can go from there."

"Detective, see what you can find in the police reports."

"Sounds good." Vance nodded.

As he was fishing his medallion from his pocket, Giles frowned and looked at Derek. "While you're looking through those reports, look at the medical examiner's report on Amelia's body. I'd like to know what the dried leaves Lenox saw the killer sprinkling on Amelia were."

"I'll get right on it. What will you be doing?"

Giles waved the medallion and crossed through the archway before replying. "I'm going to dig deeper into what rituals that dagger is used for." His eyes were shadowed with worry as he glanced at us.

"We need to know what we're dealing with, but if black magic is involved, this is very serious. Keep your cell phones on and stay in touch. We'll regroup and share our findings tomorrow evening. Six o'clock work for everyone?"

I took a deep breath, steeling myself for the task ahead. The night felt colder, the shadows deeper, but knowing we had a plan gave me a sense of control and kept me from panicking over the involvement of dark magic.

There was an undercurrent rippling between us as we climbed the stone stairs and made our way back to Bull Street, but the subject uppermost in all of our minds was dropped in favor of speculation about the Twilight Tavern and its patrons.

Derek and I laughed and joked and prodded Giles for answers about Reed, Dante, and all of the wondrous creatures we'd seen.

"Psychic vampires and fae..." Derek snorted and shook his head as he nudged Giles with his elbow. "It's unbelievable, and have they always lived among us?"

Giles shook his head. "No, most supernatural beings don't live with humans."

Derek frowned. "So why are those two here?"

Giles smiled, but his answers remained cryptic. "Reed and Dante have their secrets, just like everyone else."

Arriving at the Westlake Mansion, we said goodnight and parted ways. Unlocking the carriage house door, the nagging sense that we were on the verge of uncovering something far more sinister than we had imagined lingered, but as I watched Derek start his car and Giles enter the main house, some of my worry dissipated. Whatever was going on, we would face it together.

13
RESEARCH
AND
DEVELOPMENTS

S crolling through the last article, I hit the print button and walked to the circulation desk. While I waited for the librarian to deliver my copies, I considered what I'd learned about the body thefts.

Locally, ten bodies had been stolen over the last year, but a wider search revealed bodies had been going missing in Florida, South Carolina, and Georgia for over two years. Not only were they being stolen from funeral homes—the morgue and even cemeteries had been struck.

At a rough count, over one hundred bodies had been stolen, and from what I could tell, no official investigation had linked the thefts. Police reports were filed, but if there were any leads, they weren't sharing it publicly.

One of the local funeral homes had reported another theft of two bodies six weeks ago. A quick search gave me the address, and since it was just past two o'clock, I figured I had plenty of time to pay the home a visit before my meeting with Giles and Derek.

Fletcher Funeral Home was housed in a large, powder blue Victorian with gingerbread trim and a spacious front porch outfitted with wicker furniture and potted ferns. The blue siding was soothing, the seating area peaceful, and the lush landscaping muted the noise from traffic—a perfect atmosphere to welcome the bereaved.

Heels clicking on the wooden floor, I crossed to the front door and pushed the doorbell. Getting no response, I lifted the brass door knocker but still received no answer. Assuming they were closed, I skipped down the steps and headed for home, but as I reached the front gate, I heard a radio.

Curious, I tracked the music to the back of the house where I found an older man dressed in coveralls washing a black hearse.

"Excuse me," I called out, catching his attention.

He turned off the hose and wiped his hands on a rag. "Yes, ma'am? Can I help you?"

I smiled and moved closer. "Hi, I'm Lenox Grady. I'm investigating the recent body thefts and was hoping to ask you a few questions."

He nodded and offered his hand. "Nice to meet ya. I'm Mike Carlson." He let out a dry laugh and shook his head. "Sure am glad to see somebody finally takin' an interest. You a reporter?"

"Ah, something like that," I mumbled, shaking his hand firmly.

Mike didn't seem to care why I was asking. He walked over to a bench nestled beneath the portico and took a long drink from a bottle of water. After he'd swiped at his mouth, he met my gaze and then shook his head. "Stealin' bodies...you gotta be off yer rocker to go messin' with the dead like that. What you reckon they wanted them poor souls fer?"

"I'm not entirely sure yet," I admitted. "But I'm hoping you might be able to help me figure that out. When you discovered the body was missing, did you notice anything strange about the room? Any signs of a struggle or anything out of place?"

Mike scratched his head thoughtfully. "Well, now that you mention it, the room smelled funny, like burned rubber. Looked all over but didn't find no singed wires or nuthin'. Only other thing was some blood on the prep table."

"Blood?" I asked, raising an eyebrow. "That's unusual, right?"

"Yes ma'am, it sure is. When the bodies are moved in there, they already been embalmed, so there ain't supposed to be no blood," Mike explained. He looked down at the ground and sighed. "Darn shame, someone bein' so disrespectful."

"Yes, it is, and I can't imagine what those families are going through."

A respectful lull settled between us as we both considered the impact on the victims' loved ones. The silence was filled with unspoken empathy and sorrow.

Gently breaking the silence, I asked, "Is there anything else you noticed? Anything at all?"

Mike started to shake his head but then paused, his eyes widening slightly. "Oh! Almost forgot. There were dried leaves all over the floor, underneath the prep table. Never seen anything like it before."

"Dried leaves?" I repeated, my interest piqued. "Could you tell what they were?"

"Nope, just little specks. Reminded me of oregano or parsley maybe?" He huffed a laugh. "Thought it was dang strange to find 'em there and told the police, only they didn't think it was important." He peered at me. "You reckon it's got somethin' to do with them missin' bodies?"

"I don't know, Mike, but it's possible."

"Strange days all around, I reckon. Oh, and now that I think of it, there was another lady in here a while back, just after the first theft, asking questions about all this, too."

My heart skipped. "A woman?"

"Yeah, pretty redhead. She was a reporter, too. Thought it odd at the time, but now you're here asking the same kind of questions."

I bit my lip, my mind racing. "Did she say what paper she worked for?"

Mike shook his head. "Naw, she didn't, but she was mighty interested in them body snatchers."

I suppressed a shiver. That had to be Amelia. "Well, thank you, Mike. I appreciate the information."

"Whelp"—he walked over to the car and picked up the hose—"nice talkin' to ya, Ms. Lenox, but I gotta get her ready for a funeral tomorrow."

I smiled. "I understand. Thank you for taking the time to chat with me and, uh, if you think of anything else, please let me know."

"Will do, you have a nice day now!"

As I walked away from Fletcher Funeral Home, Mike's words echoed in my mind. Dried leaves like oregano or parsley... It sounded eerily similar to the herbs I'd seen the killer sprinkle over Amelia's body. And Amelia had been here, asking the same questions. A sense of dread crept over me at the realization—could the body thief be Amelia's killer?

Lost in thought, I was walking down a quiet residential street when the hair on the back of my neck stood up. I glanced around and saw nothing unusual, but the uneasy feeling grew with each step.

I'd just passed an alley when I could have sworn I heard footsteps. I turned quickly but saw nothing. Just my imagination, I tried to reassure myself.

The sun was setting, leaving too many dark and shadowed corners for my comfort. I picked up my pace, trying to talk myself off the proverbial ledge, but by the time I reached Bull Street, my heart was pounding and my imagination was running wild.

Seeing the façade of Giles's home, I broke into a run, sprinting through Monterrey Square like the hounds of hell were nipping at my heels. As I reached the front gate, I couldn't shake the feeling that someone—or something—was watching me from the shadows.

Strung tighter than a bowstring after the walk home, I made myself a sandwich and worked at convincing myself I had been imagining things.

Tucked up in my cozy apartment, I finally calmed down enough to consider what I'd learned about the funeral home thefts. The dried leaves, the smell of burned rubber, and the unexpected blood all pointed to something sinister.

Determined to piece it all together, I headed to Giles's house for our scheduled meeting. The walk across the secluded courtyard garden was less harrowing than my earlier jaunt, but I still felt a prickle of unease as I approached his back door.

Giles greeted me with a warm smile, ushering me into his study where Derek was already seated, surrounded by open books and notes. The room was filled with the comforting scent of old paper and leather, a stark contrast to the tension that hung in the air.

"Lenox, you look like you've had quite a day," Giles said, obviously noting my frazzled appearance.

"You could say that," I replied, taking a seat. "I got the articles from the library and then decided to poke around at one of the funeral homes. Learned some interesting things." Not wanting to derail our conversation, I didn't mention my walk home.

"Do tell," Derek encouraged, leaning forward.

I recounted my conversation with Mike, emphasizing the dried leaves, the strange smell, and the blood on the prep table. "It's all too similar to what I saw the killer use on Amelia," I concluded.

Giles rubbed his chin thoughtfully. "It sounds like dark magic is definitely at play here."

The room fell silent as we all absorbed the disturbing news. Derek cleared his throat and sat forward in his chair. "Okay, I get the impression that is bad but help a guy out and tell me why."

Giles adjusted his glasses and leaned back, his expression serious. "Dark magic involves the manipulation of supernatural forces for malevolent purposes. It often requires ingredients and rituals that are inherently corrupting, such as blood, grave dirt, and certain herbs."

Derek raised an eyebrow. "Oh boy, that sounds pretty serious."

Giles nodded. "It is, so we need to be careful. Now, what did the medical examiner's report say?"

Derek pulled out his notes. "They analyzed the herbs found on Amelia's body. Turns out, it's *Artemisia absinthium*." He looked up and shrugged. "No idea what that is though or whether it means anything."

Giles sat back and propped his chin on steepled hands. His brow was furrowed, and there was a hard look in his eyes, telling me he was troubled by something. A few seconds ticked by before he enlightened us.

"It's wormwood."

I frowned. "And that's bad?"

Giles nodded slowly, his expression somber. "Wormwood is a powerful herb used in dark magic rituals. Finding it in these circumstances suggests that whoever is behind this is delving into some very dangerous practices."

Derek's eyes widened. "So, what exactly does that mean for us?"

Giles took a deep breath. "It means that we need to be on our guard." He looked at Derek. "And you need some personal protection."

Derek grinned and patted his side. "My Glock is all I need."

Giles shook his head. "Not necessarily, detective. Firearms don't work on spirits."

The smile faded from Derek's face as he absorbed the implications in Giles' statement.

A slight smile curved Giles's lips as he nodded. "Just so." He clapped his hands and sat upright. "Now then, you've both done very well and combined with what I learned about the symbols on the dagger, I can make some educated guesses about what we are dealing with."

He glanced at the clock on the mantel. "However, it's almost time for you to start your tour, Lenox, so let's plan to visit Selena tomorrow morning. We'll confirm if my hunch is correct and get Derek some protection for threats of the supernatural kind."

As I rose to leave, Giles put his hand on my arm. Worry was clear in his eyes. "Lenox, be extra vigilant tonight. If someone is using dark magic, they might know we're onto them."

My mind ran back to my experiences while walking home, and a sudden sense of dread gripped me. Had the killer somehow known I was investigating and followed me? I fingered the black tourmaline pendant hanging around my neck and swallowed hard. "I will, Giles. See you both tomorrow."

The weight of urgency and the gravity of our situation pressed down on me as I left the study. A sense of racing against time gnawed at me. As I approached the gates of Colonial Park Cemetery, the shadows seemed to whisper warnings, urging me to be cautious.

14
VEXED AND HEXED

The tour went well; everyone seemed satisfied, and since I didn't encounter any ghosts, I considered the night a success. Exhausted and ready for the peace and quiet of my home, I still doubted I'd sleep well.

The meeting with Giles and Derek had left me uneasy. Coupled with the unsettling feeling that someone had followed me on my way home from the funeral parlor, I was a borderline nervous wreck. Before going to bed, I double-checked the locks on the doors and windows, all the while telling myself it was just my imagination running wild.

Despite my frayed nerves, I was asleep within minutes of my head hitting the pillow.

The gallery is packed with people clamoring for my attention, but I only have eyes for a series of paintings hanging on the back wall. I wind my way through the throng and breathe a sigh of relief when I'm standing before them.

I study a scene of a marsh at sunset, its gold and purple hues casting a weathered cabin in multicolored shadows. A dilapidated dock juts out from shore, a ramshackle skiff bobbing with the current. The idyllic image yearns to soothe me, but my nerves are stretched taut; "I must hide" runs through my mind on an endless loop.

A couple sidles up to view the painting. Not wanting to be bothered, I move to the second landscape. The light of a full moon dances across the ocean, casting shadows over the forest that runs along the edge of the beach. A bonfire, half-hidden by the stand of pines, turns the surrounding sand to liquid gold, and I can almost feel the heat seeping into my bones. I reach out, as if to warm my hands, and the world tilts.

Suddenly, I'm leaning against a gnarled oak, the pounding surf synchronizing with my racing heart. Hide, hide, my mind screams. The sound of raised voices yelling my name draws nearer. Trembling, I gather the full skirts of my ballgown and run, only to trip over a tree root.

Face down in the pine straw, I struggle to rise—too late! Snapping branches and shuffling footsteps are coming closer...

Pulse pounding in my ears, I jolted upright and shook off the dregs of my nightmare. I reached for the glass of water on my nightstand, thankful I'd awakened before whatever was chasing me could make its appearance.

Blowing out a breath, I fluffed my pillow and started to lay back down when a faint noise froze me in place. My muscles tensed, my heart racing. *It's just your imagination*, I told myself, *remnants of your dream—*

A sudden, sharp sound of breaking glass shattered the silence. My heart leaped into my throat, and I bolted upright, ears straining to catch any other sounds. A scuffling noise came from the kitchen.

Someone was in the house! Shaking like a leaf, I pressed my ear to the door, hoping to convince myself it was just the wind or my overactive imagination. But the unmistakable sound of footsteps shuffling across the hardwood floors shattered that hope.

My breath caught, and my mind went blank. *What should I do?* I looked around for a weapon, anything to defend myself, when a low moan echoed off the walls, priming me into action.

Heart pounding, I pressed my ear to the door again, hoping to hear the intruder leaving. The footsteps grew louder, closer. My pulse quickened. I needed to get out, now.

Frantically, I considered my options. Whoever it was, they were in my living room, eliminating escape through the front or French doors. My heart pounded louder in my ears with each passing second. Dark spots were forming on the edges of my vision—I was about to pass out.

Think, Lenox, think!

Forcing myself to take several deep breaths, I glanced around my small bedroom. The closet? Bathroom? Under the bed? No. Then, a branch scratched against the windowpane, and my eyes went wide.

The window!

Grabbing my phone, I shoved the window frame open and stuck my head out. The drop was about five feet—maybe I'd sprain an ankle, but it was my only option.

The knob on my bedroom door rattled.

Without another thought, I jumped.

Wincing as my bare feet sank into the pine straw, I sprinted across the courtyard to Giles's house and banged on the door.

"Come on, come on..." I looked over my shoulder, expecting an attack. I raised my hand to knock again when the door creaked open.

"Lenox? What's wrong?"

"Someone's in my apartment!" I gasped.

Brows rising to meet his hairline, Giles grabbed a walking stick and stepped onto the porch. "Call Detective Vance. I'll check it out."

I dialed Vance as Giles hurried across the courtyard.

"Vance," came a groggy voice.

"Derek! Someone is in my house and Giles is going over to—"

"What? No! Tell him to wait. I'm on my way. Call 911!"

I dialed emergency services as I ran across the garden, calling for Giles. I caught him just outside the front door.

"Derek says to wait—"

"911, what's your emergency?"

Tugging on Giles's arm, I led him back to the main house as I explained the situation to the operator.

"I'm sending help. Please stay on the line."

Moments later, Derek's car screeched to a halt in front of the house. He rushed over, gun drawn, his expression tense. A couple of police cruisers followed closely behind, red and blue lights flashing.

"Where are they?" Derek asked, scanning the area.

"They're inside," I whispered, pointing toward the carriage house. "Be careful, Derek."

The police officers joined Derek, and together they approached the door, their flashlights cutting through the darkness. Giles and I watched from a safe distance, our breaths held.

A few tense moments passed before Derek signaled us to come closer. "It's clear," he called out. "But the kitchen window is broken, and there are signs someone was definitely here."

Giles and I followed him inside. A musty smell of rot hit us immediately.

"What's that smell? It's like something died in here," I said, wrinkling my nose.

Giles's eyes narrowed as he inhaled deeply. "Rotting flesh," he confirmed, moving into the kitchen. His gaze swept the room, then he gasped and crouched down to inspect something on the tile.

"What is that?" I asked, kneeling beside him. Something gray and powdery was sprinkled across several tiles. "Looks like ash."

Giles shook his head but didn't comment, rising to inspect the counter and windowsill. "Ah, I was afraid of that." Giles muttered, his expression growing darker.

I leaned closer to the counter and saw a dried puddle of something that was colored a dull black. There were flakes of dark green surrounding it with more scattered on the windowsill and sink.

"What is all this, Giles?"

He leaned down and picked up a pinch of the dust, rubbing it between his fingers. "Dirt. And..." He nodded toward the counter. "If, as I suspect, that is black candle wax, and those flecks in the sink are herbs, then there is a hex bag somewhere in this house."

"A hex bag? I don't understand—"

"Search the apartment. Derek?" Giles hollered. "Take the living room. Lenox, check your bedroom." He started opening cupboards. "You're looking for a small cloth pouch. Probably black or dark purple, with symbols drawn on it."

This was all too much. I'd been dragged out of a sound sleep, scared out of my wits, and now there was some kind of hex in my house? Bewildered, I watched Giles tear my kitchen apart as my mind tried to make sense of it all.

"Lenox!" His sharp tone snapped me out of my stupor.

"Move. It is essential that we find that bag!"

The anxiety in his voice propelled me toward my room. I was rifling through my dresser drawers when I heard Giles holler that if we found the bag, we were not to touch it.

Was this thing that dangerous? My stomach churned, and I became more cautious as I continued my search.

I'd searched my closet, bathroom, and dressers without finding anything. Exhaustion weighed heavily on me, and I sank onto the bed, yawning. As I started to stretch out, I noticed black smudges on my pillowcase.

I was reaching out to dust them off when alarm bells went off in my head. Backing away without taking my eyes off the smudges, I stopped at the bedroom door and yelled for Giles. A split second later, both men were beside me.

"What is it?" Giles asked.

My hand shook as I pointed toward my pillow. "That dirt wasn't there when I went to bed."

Giles's expression darkened as he moved closer to examine it. "You did the right thing by not touching it, Lenox." He leaned in, careful not to make contact. "These smudges are from the dirt we found on the kitchen floor, which leads me to believe the hex is under the pillow."

Derek stepped forward, his eyes narrowing. "So what exactly does that mean for her?"

"It means," Giles said, straightening up, "that the curse can activate with touch. We need to handle this carefully." He turned to me, his voice firm but reassuring. "Lenox, I need a plastic bag. And kitchen tongs."

I nodded, my nerves making my movements jerky as I retrieved the items. Giles took the tongs and carefully lifted the pillow, revealing a small, black cloth pouch with dark symbols scrawled on it.

"Just as I thought," he said grimly, placing it gently into the plastic bag. "We'll put this in the freezer and take it to Selena first thing in the morning. The cold should help to neutralize it temporarily."

Giles sealed the plastic bag and turned to me. "You're staying with me tonight, no arguments."

I nodded, too shaken to protest. Derek looked between us, concern etched on his face. "What about the rest of her apartment? Is it safe?"

Giles nodded. "The hex bag is the main concern. With it contained, Lenox should be safe now. However, the apartment will have to be cleansed and protected with wards. I'll consult with Selena tomorrow."

Derek exhaled heavily. "Alright. I'll make sure everything is secure before we leave."

As the reality of the night's events sank in, a wave of nausea hit me. Whoever was behind this wasn't just practicing dark magic—they were coming for me.

15

DARK TIDINGS

True to his word, Giles was pounding on the door to his guest room at the crack of dawn.

"Lenox? Rise and shine, we need to visit Selena."

Groaning, I sat up and shook myself awake. "I'm up, give me a few minutes."

"Ten minutes. I'll be waiting at the front door."

Ugh. *No pressure!* Grumbling, I forced myself out of bed and stumbled into the bathroom. Necessities seen to, I splashed water on my face, brushed my teeth, and then pulled on a pair of jeans and a T-shirt. A baseball cap to hide my bedhead, and I was ready—well, ready to look awake, at least.

Half-asleep, I managed to get down the stairs without breaking any limbs and found Giles impatiently waiting with a small red cooler in his hand.

"There you are." He pulled the door open and motioned for me to precede him. "Ah, a beautiful spring morning, perfect for a brisk walk. Let's get going, Derek is meeting us there."

Not up to arguing, I trailed after him as he set off across Monterrey Square. When we exited the small park, the smell of coffee and freshly baked bread hit my nose, making my stomach growl.

"Giles"—we were half a block from Marco's Bistro and all I could think about was food and tea—"can't we at least have breakfast first?"

Giles shook his head. "Getting protection on the property is top priority."

I frowned. "Didn't you say you have wards on the mansion?"

"Indeed, I do. However, those protections were put in place years ago, and they weren't meant for this kind of threat."

My stomach churned. "Uh, what kind of threat are we dealing with, Giles?"

He hesitated for a moment, then replied, "I have a strong suspicion, but I'll wait for Selena to confirm. Now, do hurry. Derek is probably already there." He raised the cooler and shook it gently. "And I don't want this hex bag to thaw." He gave me a sideways glance, a hint of a smile playing on his lips. "If you hurry, I'll treat you to breakfast afterward."

That perked me up a bit, and I picked up my pace. We arrived at Selena's shop to find Derek already waiting outside, leaning against his car with a coffee cup in hand.

"Morning," Derek greeted us, offering a small nod. "Ready to find out what we're dealing with?"

Selena opened the door before we could answer, her keen eyes taking in our expressions. "Come in, come in." She came over to me as I crossed the threshold and took my hands, staring into my eyes.

"Ah, chile, ya gave too much of yerself away." She smiled and scurried around the counter.

I quirked a brow and glanced at Giles, silently asking if he'd told her about my energy transfer with Amelia. He shook his head and I sighed; it was too early to ponder how Selena could know, so I just accepted the brown vial she handed me.

"Now den, shake it up real good and ya take a tablespoon of dis tonic once a day for five days or until it's gone."

I nodded. "Thanks." I held the bottle up to the light. It was cloudy, with bits of something on the bottom of the glass. "Um, what's in it?"

Selena's lips twitched and her brown eyes danced with laughter. "Eye of newt, wing of a bat, and just a pinch of dragon's breath..." She winked as Giles laughed.

"Nah, I'm just foolin' wit ya. Dis is a restorative elixir made from ginseng, nettle, licorice root, and a few things my nana taught me."

Grinning, I slipped the vial into my pocket. I was about to ask how she knew I needed the tonic when Giles cleared his throat.

"Selena, thank you for opening early for us. I'm afraid we need your help. There was a break-in at Lenox's place last night. They left a hex bag." He offered her the cooler. "We found it under Lenox's pillow. I stored it in the freezer. Can you neutralize it? We suspect it's connected to a murder investigation with paranormal origins."

Selena's eyes widened. She took the cooler and set it on her workbench. "A hex bag, you say? Dis ain't good, but ya did right to put it in the cold." She waved her hand for us to follow. "Let's see what we can do."

She picked up the cooler and led us to the back of the shop, where she had an altar set up. The air was thick with the scent of sage and other herbs. She gestured for us to sit while she gathered her supplies.

"You need to purify your property. Smudge wit de sage and den put da salt down, all around any openin' to de outside," Selena began, her hands moving swiftly as she spoke. "I'll give ya some protection charms to hang 'round de house. And y'all should paint de haint blue on de doors and porch ceilings. Keeps de spirits out."

Giles nodded; his expression serious. "The wards on the main house need strengthening too. They were put in place years ago for a different kind of threat."

Selena glanced at him sharply. "You shoulda done dat a long time ago, Giles. Times change, threats change."

He sighed. "You're right, of course."

She handed him several bundles of sage, a large jar of salt, and a bag of charms. Once we had the items to protect our homes, she prepared her altar.

With the supplies ready, Selena turned her attention to the hex bag. She grabbed a bundle of sage leaves and struck a match. As soon as the leaves were burning, she blew them out and waved the herbs over the bag and around her workspace.

"Now den, everything is nice and clean." She set the smoldering leaves on a ceramic dish and turned to a series of candles aligned on a shelf behind her. "White candles to purify and protect and..." Her hand hovered over a jet-black candle.

She turned toward Giles and cocked an eyebrow. "Ya want me to send dis back to its maker?"

Giles's brows shot up and he cocked his head to the side. "Well now, I hadn't thought about that." He stared off into the distance for a second, then glanced at Derek and me. "Whoever is behind this will know we are onto them if Selena sends the curse back. Should we lay our cards on the table or keep the element of surprise?"

I shrugged. "Don't look at me..."

Derek crossed his arms, his brow furrowed in thought. "As much as I want to give them a taste of their own medicine, I think we should keep the element of surprise. It gives us the upper hand. We need to gather more information and figure out who we're dealing with before they know we're onto them."

Giles nodded, appreciating the practical approach. "Very well, we'll keep the surprise then." He looked at Selena. "Just deactivate it for now, thank you."

"As you wish." She left the black candle on the shelf and turned back to the altar. "Now to take de mojo out of dis foul creation."

Donning a pair of surgical gloves, she removed the hex bag from the cooler and carefully cut it open, letting the contents spill out onto the white tablecloth.

The air around the table seemed to shift, turning hazy. The items pulsed with malevolent energy; coldness settled into my bones, and a weight dragged at me, like I was being held down by cement shoes.

I wrapped my arms around myself and watched as Selena sifted and sorted.

"Ah, dey used bones. Look at dis, Giles." She motioned him closer and cautioned him not to touch.

"Hmmm, there are runes carved on it. Someone took considerable time with these."

"Aye, I don't recognize dis language." Selena glanced at Giles. "Do you know what it says?"

He drew a deep breath and shook his head. "Unfortunately, no." He stared at the bones, then straightened. "We'll need to return to the Twilight Tavern. It's possible Reed might know."

The negative energy swirling around the hex bag had already sent unease coursing through me, but seeing the worry etched on Giles's face only heightened my anxiety.

"Uh, you can stop it though, right? Whatever it's meant to do?"

Giles flashed a weak smile that did nothing to alleviate my fears.

"Selena's spell should counter the curse, but we'll need to remain vigilant."

Selena nodded. "Aye, no need to be frettin' just yet, chile. We goin' stop dis mess right now."

She put action to her words and anointed the white candle with oil. Lighting it, she began to chant.

"By candle's light and sacred flame,

I call upon the ancient name.

Purify this hex, undo its might,

Turn dark to light, restore what's right.

With earth and air, with fire and sea,

I break this curse and set you free.

So mote it be."

I gasped as the air shifted again and the energy dissipated. "Selena, that's amazing!"

She smiled. "Aye, chile, the power of good always triumphs." Her smile faded as she glanced down at the strangely marked bones. "But dis..." She looked at Giles. "Not knowin' what dis says, I can't promise it's inactive."

He dipped his head. "Understood."

Selena looked at Derek and me. "Until we know what we're dealin' with, ya need to take extra precautions. Make sure your homes are secured wit da salt and paint and hang da charms I gave ya. Carry salt and these iron nails wit ya; they can help ward off malevolent entities."

We took the nails and nodded that we understood.

Selena clapped her hands. "Good. Now, what's dis about a murder?"

Giles explained about Amelia, what I had seen, and showed her my drawing of the dagger. He also mentioned Reed's identification of the dagger being used in dark magic and the wormwood sprinkled on Amelia's body and in my apartment.

Selena's expression grew more grave with each detail. "Dis is a ritual for animatin' da dead." She pointed at the strange symbols carved on the dagger's hilt.

My eyes widened as I gasped. "What? You mean like a zombie?"

Derek scoffed. "Oh come on, are you saying there are zombies walking around Savannah?"

Selena directed a hard stare at Derek. "Dat is exactly what I'm sayin', and you mock at yer peril." She looked at Giles. "You don't seem surprised."

He sighed and shook his head. "No, I had come to the conclusion we were dealing with a necromancer, but I'd hoped to be wrong."

"Aye, dis is bad juju..."

The hair on my neck rose as I heard the fear in Selena's voice. "Um, but we can stop them, right?" I looked around the shop. "You have something we can use to...to..."

She shook her head. "Nah, chile, ain't no herbs or roots goin' to counter dark magic like dis. Whoever dis is, dey're powerful and dangerous."

The room fell silent as the weight of her words sank in. We had suspected dark magic, but a necromancer was far worse than I had imagined. We were up against someone who could control the dead, and that was a terrifying thought.

Selena looked at each of us in turn, her gaze steady and strong. "Strengthen de wards, stay protected, and keep your eyes open. Dis fight ain't gonna be easy."

Giles frowned. "The situation isn't hopeless, however." He looked at Selena. "First we need to ascertain what this person is using to wield their magic. We know they have stolen dead bodies. What does that tell us?"

"That they're sick and evil?"

I laughed at Derek's dry response. "That goes without saying. But since they took dead bodies, they must want them for something." I looked at Giles. "Why would they want bodies?"

Giles's expression was grim. "The only thing that comes to mind is they want an army of the undead."

I gulped. I'd been thinking that, but I hadn't wanted to put it into words. "Okay...so what would someone do with an army of dead soldiers?"

"Well, armies imply war or conquest. So, what do they want to control or rule over?"

"De world."

Eyes wide, we all looked at Selena, who shrugged. "If someone is risking dey soul practicin' dark magic, they want somethin' big. What's bigger than de world?"

Giles cocked his head to one side and stroked his goatee. "True, but I wonder..."

"What, Giles? What else could they want?"

He shook his head. "I've a hunch, but we'll need to pay another visit to the Twilight Tavern." He nodded toward a shelf full of bottles and baskets. "For now, let's finish gathering our protection supplies, and then we'll go eat. No sense worrying about the fate of humanity on an empty stomach."

We walked to Marco's Bistro, the tantalizing aroma of fresh bread and brewing coffee beckoning us. As we neared the entrance, a familiar voice called out.

"Lenox! Good morning."

I turned to see Julian, his eyes bright with curiosity and a hint of something more. "Julian, hi!" I replied, feeling a flutter of nerves and excitement.

"I hadn't heard from you, so I assumed...well, I wasn't sure if you were still interested."

My eyes widened. "Oh no, I've just been really, really busy," I explained, glancing at Giles and Derek waiting by the door. "We're helping the detective with a case. Mainly Giles, but it means I'm picking up extra tours."

Julian nodded, his gaze shifting between them and back to me. "Well, in that case, how about dinner tonight? Just us."

I hesitated for a moment, thinking of the chaos and danger surrounding us, but then I smiled. "I'd like that."

"Great. I'll pick you up at seven?"

"Seven it is."

As Julian walked away, I turned back to Giles and Derek, who were watching with amused expressions. "What?"

"Nothing," Giles said, a smile tugging at his lips. "Just remember, no matter what happens, stay vigilant."

"Always," I replied, a smile spreading across my face, my mind already jumping ahead to the evening.

We stepped into the bistro, ready to discuss our next steps over a much-needed meal. The gravity of the situation hung over us like a dark cloud. But at least we had a plan, and that gave me a small measure of comfort. We would face this threat together, and with Selena's help, we had a fighting chance.

16

DEADLY DATE

As the waiter cleared our plates, Julian reached across the table, covering my hand. "I'm glad you could make it tonight."

I smiled. "Me too."

As I glanced down at our hands, a glint of metal caught my eye. On his ring finger, Julian wore a striking signet ring—a serpent devouring its own tail, the Ouroboros. My breath caught in my throat. I knew this symbol. Not just from my nightmares but from the gate I'd seen with Giles.

"That ring," I said, my voice barely more than a whisper. "Where did you get it?"

Julian's eyebrows raised slightly, and I noticed a flicker of something in his eyes—surprise, perhaps, or something else. "It's been in my family for years, passed down to the oldest son. Why?"

I leaned closer, studying the symbol. "I've seen this before. In a dream...and then again, on a gate in the city. What does it mean?"

Julian raised an eyebrow, then smiled as if a memory had surfaced. "Of course, that's right. You added it to your painting at the gallery event. Remember? The doll in your still life?"

My eyes widened. He was right—I had painted the Ouroboros onto the doll. But why? I hadn't thought much of it at the time. It had just felt...right. But now, seeing it again, I couldn't shake the growing sense that this symbol meant something more than coincidence.

"But what does it mean?" I pressed, my gaze narrowing as I studied Julian's face for any hint of recognition or significance.

Julian shrugged casually, though the way his thumb traced the edge of the ring suggested something more. "It's a common symbol," he said, his voice light, almost dismissive. "The Ouroboros represents the cycle of life, creation and destruction, things like that. Lots of families use it as a crest or a mark of tradition."

I frowned, not quite satisfied with his explanation. "It just seems strange to keep seeing it. First in my dream, then on the gate, and now here—on your ring."

Julian squeezed my hand, offering a reassuring smile. "Lenox, sometimes our minds make connections because we're looking for patterns. It's probably nothing more than a coincidence."

Maybe he was right. But deep down, a part of me wasn't so sure. There was something unsettling about how the Ouroboros kept finding its way into my life, and Julian's nonchalance only heightened my suspicion.

"But I've seen it twice now—once in a dream and once in real life. Are you sure there isn't more to it?"

Julian's eyes softened as he squeezed my hand gently. "Lenox, symbols can be powerful in their own right, but they're often just that—symbols. Maybe you're just noticing it because it's caught your eye before."

Maybe he's right, I thought, trying not to overthink it. No need to make a big deal out of it. I nodded slowly. "Maybe," I conceded. "But it's still strange, don't you think?"

He shrugged, his smile returning. "Life is full of strange coincidences. Now, how about another glass of wine? I'd love to hear more about your ghost stories."

I laughed, deciding to let the subject drop. The night was too beautiful to dwell on curious family heirlooms. I launched into a story from my latest tour, watching Julian's face light up with interest.

The city's vibrant nightlife faded into the background, as I found myself captivated by Julian's presence. He leaned back, taking in the bustling atmosphere.

"Evenings like these remind me why I love Savannah—the vibrant life, the art, the stories. It's the same passion I try to bring to the gallery."

"So you grew up here and took over the family business?"

Julian laughed. "No, my family's in banking. I left to pursue art. It wasn't easy, but they respected my decision, eventually."

"That sounds tough. How did you manage?" I asked.

"My grandfather cut me off financially. It taught me resilience... and creativity."

I smiled. "What drove you to art? Are you an artist?"

"My grandmother was the artist," Julian explained. "Her paintings were forgotten until we found them after she passed. They inspired me to open the gallery."

"You've turned personal history into something meaningful for others," I said, impressed.

Julian smiled, a look of understanding passing briefly over his features. "Art has a way of speaking to us, doesn't it? Sometimes, it feels like it's reaching out, connecting threads of the past and present."

Curiosity stirred as I pondered Julian's story. There was something about the idea of hidden talents and unexplored passions that resonated deeply. My mind flashed to the night I'd attended his art party.

I'd lost myself in painting that night. The brush in my hand had felt so familiar, comforting; like I'd finally come home. Could I have had a similar passion in my forgotten past?

The thought surfaced briefly, a whisper of possibility, before I gently pushed it away. It was doubtful my past held anything so glamorous.

I smiled and focused on Julian. "That's a beautiful legacy to carry forward."

"I try." He smiled and reached across the table, taking my hand. "But, enough about me. Tell me all about the beautiful and beguiling Lenox Grady and her fascinating profession."

Julian's question caught me off guard. I laughed nervously, searching for the right words. How could I explain the amnesia and ghost chatting without sounding completely off my rocker?

I bit my lip and searched for words. "Um, I met Giles shortly after moving here." I shrugged. "He—uh, needed help, and I was intrigued by Savannah's history."

"I've heard good things, so clearly, you have a knack for it," Julian remarked, squeezing my hand gently. "Everyone has a beginning somewhere, right?"

"Right." I let out a breath, relieved my story didn't reveal my weird abilities or lack of memories. "What about you? Any ghosts in your line of work?"

Julian laughed. "Only the ghosts of past critics."

The server brought the bill. Julian settled it and then suggested a walk along River Street to walk off our dinner. I slipped my hand into his as we stood. "I'd love to."

Stepping outside, a strange tension prickled in the air. The moon's reflection on the river seemed unnaturally bright, casting long, dark shadows. A rising sense of unease settled over me, though I couldn't say why. I tried to focus on Julian's voice, but something felt...off.

As we walked, the distant laughter and music seemed to echo strangely, almost distorted. A cool breeze swept in from the river, carrying a scent of salt and something else—something that made the hair on the back of my neck stand up. I shook my head, trying to dismiss the dread that had settled in my stomach.

Despite the tension, the sound of distant music and the chatter of people enjoying the nightlife created a pleasant backdrop. The river shimmered under the soft glow of the full moon, and with each step, I willed myself to relax.

Maybe it was just my imagination or the lingering thoughts of the ring. I took a deep breath, letting the fresh night air fill my lungs, and tried to let go of my misgivings.

Julian's ring caught my eye again, the Ouroboros glinting in the moonlight. I resisted the urge to ask more about it, sensing that Julian wasn't ready—or willing—to share its full significance. His earlier deflection was subtle, but I hadn't missed it. What was he hiding?

I gave his hand a gentle squeeze, deciding to push the questions from my mind. Tonight was about enjoying the moment, not probing into mysteries. Julian seemed to sense my distraction and gently nudged me. "Penny for your thoughts?"

I forced a smile. "Just enjoying the night," I said, sidestepping my curiosity for now. "Tell me more about your family. You mentioned earlier that the ring is an heirloom."

He chuckled softly, his posture relaxing. "Oh, my family's history isn't nearly as exciting as your ghost stories, I assure you."

I smiled, letting him change the subject. But as we continued our walk, my mind kept drifting back to the Ouroboros, its presence nagging at me like an unsolved puzzle.

Deciding the evening was too perfect to mar by prying into his business, I considered the ghost stories I'd researched, looking for one that was tied to River Street.

The air by the river was cooler, the city sounds fading next to the lapping water. Our walk took us toward the east end of the river, near the waving girl statue. The dim lighting and tree cover were perfect for a ghostly tale about Florence Martus, the real-life waving girl.

"You know about Florence, the sister of the lighthouse keeper on Elba Island, right?"

Julian nodded as I started telling him about the waving girl. "It's thought she waved at the ships because she was waiting—" My words faltered as an unsettling sensation crawled up my spine.

I knew what that feeling meant. Trying to keep Julian unaware, I continued the story, but my senses were on high alert. There was a shift in the air, a prickling sensation that told me something was very wrong. And then I saw her—Amelia Walsh's shimmering form, just beyond the edge of the light.

"Lenox," Amelia's voice was a whisper, carried on the wind. "He knows you are here!"

I frowned and shook my head, hoping Amelia understood I wasn't free to talk. Julian was still looking out at the water while I prattled on with more ghost stories, but Amelia wasn't taking the hint!

She drifted closer and whispered, "Run!" Before winking out of sight.

My eyes widened. I looked around but saw nothing alarming. Maybe there was a loose connection in the spirit world? A gust of wind rustled the trees and carried a stench like raw sewage. It hit my nose, making me want to gag.

Julian sniffed and looked toward the ports. "Whew, the paper mill must be running overtime tonight!"

"Mmm, it's pretty bad." I murmured. My internal alarm bells were ringing. First Amelia's warning and now this. The cheerful sounds of laughter and clinking glasses around us seemed to muffle, replaced by an almost tangible silence that pressed in from all sides. The air felt thick and almost buzzed with electricity but Julian seemed oblivious to it.

Something was definitely wrong and it wasn't the paper mill across the river. I glanced around, my heart pounding, trying to pinpoint the source of my unease.

An unsettling weight settled in my stomach as I scanned the small park across from the waterfront. The shadows seemed to stretch and twist, warping the reality around us.

"Lenox, what's wrong?" Julian asked, concern lacing his voice.

I shook my head, not wanting to alarm him though I was unable to shake the feeling that something was very wrong. "I don't know. I just feel a bit odd..."

Before Julian could respond, the shadows in the park came to life. My heart pounded in my chest as grotesque figures began to emerge from a copse of trees.

Their rotting flesh and hollow eyes left no doubt—they were zombies! My mind raced and instinct took over. Thinking fast, I tugged on Julian's hand, drawing him back the way we'd come.

He quirked a brow but followed my lead. "What's the matter? Did you manage to spook yourself with the ghost stories?"

His green eyes sparkled as he teased me. I glanced toward the park, the minions were slow, but they'd reach us in minutes. "Uh... something like that." I forced a laugh and increased my pace. "It's kind of cold near the river. Why don't we—"

A menacing groan rang out. "What was that?" Julian jerked his head toward the river.

"Um, I don't know. Maybe a 'gator?" I gripped his hand tighter and pulled him back toward the populated part of River Street. Thankfully, he bought my explanation and followed my lead.

"I guess. Wouldn't have thought they'd be so loud."

Another moan, followed by a scream stopped us in our tracks. "What the—"

Julian started to turn around when a couple ran past us.

"Run! It's zombies!"

"Come on, Julian, let's go back to the—"

"Zombies?" He rolled his eyes and allowed me to lead him. "They've watched too many movies or hit the frozen daquiri bar one too many times."

"Yeah." I laughed though I couldn't quite hide the nervousness in my voice. "That must be it." I shivered and darted a look over my shoulder.

There'd been two rotting bodies shuffling toward us but they must have called for reinforcements, because I now counted at least eight and movement in the darkness behind them suggested there were more.

I was jerked to a stop as Julian froze mid-step, his eyes wide and unblinking. My heart started pounding in my chest. "Julian?" I waved my hand in front of his face. "Julian, can you hear me?" No response. It was as if he was frozen.

"What's going on?" My heart was racing and gooseflesh peppered my arms.

Before I could process what was happening, Reed and Dante appeared along with a man I vaguely recalled seeing behind the bar at the tavern. Callum, Reed had called him.

He was murmuring a chant, his eyes glowing with a vibrant blue light. The air around him shimmered and seemed to bend, casting an unnatural stillness over the area. It was as if he had placed a bubble around us, distorting time and space to keep the horrors at bay.

Reed strode toward the animated corpses. He mumbled something and a ball of white light appeared in his hand. He threw it at the zombies and then glanced back at me.

I watched in stunned silence as three zombies exploded in a cloud of smoke; my mind unable to grasp the surreal sight.

Everything around me felt distant and unreal, like a scene from a nightmare.

"Lenox, get out of here," he commanded, his voice steady and composed.

Reed's sharp command pierced through the fog, jolting me back to the present. I blinked and looked at him, trying to make sense of what he'd said.

Glancing over my shoulder, I saw Julian still frozen in place, his eyes wide and unblinking. "I can't, something is wrong with Julian!" I turned back to him, trying to shake him into moving.

"Callum is freezing time to keep the humans unaware," Reed explained, his voice tight with concentration. "We need to handle this quickly."

Eyes wide, I followed the line of his gaze and realized the handful of people in the area were all like Julian, standing at attention, staring into space.

Dante rushed by me, moving with predatory grace. He leaped into the air and kicked a zombie away from Reed. As his feet touched the ground, he turned in a wide arc. Using two short swords, he cut off its head before diving into the middle of the pack.

Reed continued to cast spells while Callum kept time stopped. I watched in awe as they fought off the minions, their coordinated attacks displaying a level of skill and power that was both mesmerizing and terrifying.

I stood by helplessly, my nerves fraying with each passing second as I watched the battle unfold. Fear clawed at my insides, my breath coming in shallow gasps. "What can I do?" I shouted, desperate to help.

My mind raced through possibilities, but I was paralyzed by the sheer terror of the situation. These creatures were not just figments of horror stories—they were real, and they were here.

Reed glanced at me briefly, his expression stern. "Stay back, Little Spark. This fight is ours."

I scowled. "No way I'm just standing around," I muttered, scanning for something—anything—I could use as a weapon.

"Lenox."

I jumped and turned around as Callum whispered my name.

He was focusing intently on maintaining the time freeze. Sweat poured down his face and his breathing was shaky.

"Do you need help?"

"Keep an eye on the humans," he finally managed through gritted teeth. "Make sure no zombies get near them."

Okay, that was something I could do.

Nodding, I scanned the battleground. Julian was safely behind me but a couple standing near the river weren't so lucky. Three zombies were shuffling toward them and both Reed and Dante were engaged.

I wasn't sure what the undead would do if they caught up with the humans but I darn sure didn't want to find out. I had to stop them, but what could I use?

My gaze landed on a metal trashcan. The necromancer's minions were unsteady on their feet. If I could slow them down, it might give Dante and Reed more time to send them to hell.

Out of any better ideas, I sprinted over to the can. It was heavy and full of garbage but, after a lot of grunts and swearing, I managed to get it onto its side. The zombies were closer to the couple now and I had one shot to stop them.

Gritting my teeth, I shoved the can until it was lined up and then, using every bit of strength I had, I sent it rolling down the sidewalk with an unholy clamor.

The zombies went tumbling. "Well done, Lenox!" Dante let out a laugh and rushed over to finish them off.

Seeing no further threat to the humans, I returned to Callum's side.

"Almost done?" Callum's voice was strained, his face pale and covered in sweat. "I can't hold it much longer."

My eyes widened at his words. "There are still about ten more zombies!" I cried. "What's wrong, Callum? How can I help?"

He panted heavily, barely able to speak. "Running out of energy..."

I gasped. If he stopped manipulating time the humans would wake up and be right in the thick of things! He needed to keep the humans frozen. What could I—an idea popped into my head.

"Hold on, Callum," I murmured as I placed my hands on his shoulders.

When I'd helped Amelia, it had exhausted me, but it couldn't be helped; there was no way I wanted to explain to Julian and the others why River Street was filled with animated rotting corpses.

I concentrated on gathering my life force and mentally shoved it out through my palms. The sensation was immediate. A sharp pull, like a thread being yanked from deep within me, followed by a slow burn that spread through my veins.

I gritted my teeth, pushing through the discomfort as my energy poured out of me. His breathing steadied, but my own strength was waning.

The world around me began to blur. My vision grew hazy, the edges of my sight tinged with a soft, shimmering light. I tried to stay focused, to keep my energy flowing, but I was so tired...so weak... then it happened.

A flicker. A glimpse of something else—something beyond this world.

My eyes widened. What I saw wasn't River Street. The cobblestones beneath my feet seemed to vanish, replaced by a dark, mist-covered landscape. Twisted trees loomed in the distance, their branches clawing at a blood-red sky.

I could hear whispers—faint, ghostly voices carried on a cold, biting wind. It felt like I was standing at the edge of two worlds, one foot in each, the boundary between them thin and fragile.

"What...is this?" I whispered, the words barely audible even to myself.

The air around me seemed to ripple, like the surface of a disturbed pond. There was a powerful pull, like a magnetic force drawing me toward the strange landscape.

Fear coiled in my stomach, but there was something strangely familiar about it, as if I'd been there before, or was meant to go. The whispers grew louder, more insistent, calling to me, urging me to step through.

My hands slipped from Callum's shoulders as my concentration wavered. A strange warmth made my palms itch, like I was holding onto something hot and electric. A faint, swirling distortion began to form in the air beside me—a ripple, a tear, almost like a window into another world.

"Lenox!" Callum's voice broke through the fog in my mind, sharp and urgent. He grabbed my arm and gave me a rough shake. "Stay with me! Focus!"

His words snapped me back to reality. I blinked and the world snapped back into sharp focus, the cobblestones beneath my feet solid and real once more.

The whispers were gone, replaced by the shouts and sounds of battle. The strange shimmering window disappeared as quickly as it had appeared, leaving nothing but a lingering sense of unease in its wake.

"I...I saw something," I muttered, my voice shaky. "Another place..."

Callum's grip tightened. "Focus, Lenox! I need your energy... just a little longer!"

I shook my head, trying to clear the lingering whispers from my mind. "Right...right," I stammered, refocusing on Callum. I pushed everything else aside—the fear, the confusion, the strange vision—and poured the last of my energy into him, feeling it flow like a river from me to him.

My legs were trembling, my body weak, but I forced myself to keep going, to keep pushing forward. Whatever that vision was, whatever I'd seen...it would have to wait. Right now, I needed to survive.

Refreshed by my energy, Callum maintained the time freeze and Reed and Dante dispatched the remaining zombies. Finally, the last of the undead fell, and the oppressive darkness lifted.

Reed signaled to Callum. With a whoosh of breath he released his hold and collapsed to the pavement.

"Callum!" I knelt beside him, searching for a pulse. It was there, but weak. "Reed! Callum needs help!"

Reed and Dante came running. They were in the process of lifting their friend when Julian woke up.

He blinked, shaking his head as if waking from a dream. "What happened?" he asked, looking down at Callum.

I glanced at Reed, who shrugged. *Great, no help there!*

"Um, I'm not sure, but I think this guy had too much to drink." I replied, trying to sound nonchalant, though my voice wavered. "It...it's getting late; we probably should head home." I managed to stammer.

Julian nodded, still looking puzzled. He frowned at Callum passed out on the sidewalk and then shook his head. "Yeah, probably a good idea."

Reed muttered under his breath that they were taking Callum to Giles's house. I gave a quick nod and then slipped my hand into Julian's.

The drain from giving Callum energy was catching up to me. Every step felt like wading through quicksand, my limbs heavy and sluggish.

Talking was an effort, each word like a burden on my tongue, and I wasn't at all sure I could summon enough strength to make it home. But with no other option, I gritted my teeth and forced my legs to move.

We climbed the bluff to Bay Street, and a sense of exhaustion seemed to settle on my shoulders. First the break-in at my apartment, then the hex bag, and now the vision I'd seen while helping Callum—that strange, otherworldly landscape.

What was it? Why did it feel so real? The necromancer's attention was focused on me, as if I were a magnet drawing him closer. Twice, they'd failed to harm me, but my instincts screamed that they wouldn't stop there.

A sense of impending danger gnawed at me; something about all of this felt oddly familiar, as if I was inching closer to an unseen truth. I fingered the black tourmaline under my shirt and prayed it would keep me safe from whatever came next.

When we reached my apartment, Julian turned to face me. "I had a wonderful evening," he said softly.

"Me too," I replied, feeling a warmth spread through me. He leaned in, and I met him halfway. Our lips touched, and for a moment, the world and all the fear of the necromancer fell away.

Breathless, we broke apart. I started to invite him in for a nightcap when Giles's voice rang out.

"Lenox, we need to talk." He stood at the edge of the courtyard; his expression serious.

I sighed, knowing the moment was over but grateful for the brief connection Julian and I had shared. Julian smirked and stepped back. "I have a strong sense of déjà vu."

I grinned. "Yeah, I'm sorry." I nodded toward Giles. "Must be something to do with his research for the police. I'd better go."

Julian nodded. "I'll see you soon?"

"Absolutely," I replied. I stood on tiptoe and pressed a soft kiss to his lips. "Thanks again for a perfect evening."

I watched Julian until he stepped through the gate and then made my way to the main house. I smirked. So much for a romantic evening but, at least this time, I got my kiss.

17

FORGING ALLIANCES

I stood outside Giles' study, still feeling the aftereffects of giving Callum energy. Selena's energy-restoring elixir had helped, but I was far from fully recovered. I took a deep breath and downed another tablespoon from the small vial I carried. The tonic wasn't a cure-all, but it gave me just enough of a boost to keep me from falling flat on my face.

Giles' study was a cozy dark-paneled room at the front of the house. Floor-to-ceiling bookshelves were packed with leather-bound volumes along with curiosities from his world travels. It had become my favorite room while studying for my tour guide exam.

A leather sofa, currently bearing Callum's limp form, stood opposite a roaring fire. Dante and Reed occupied wing chairs flanking the fireplace, while Giles pored over a thick tome at his desk. Derek paced so hard it was a wonder he hadn't worn a groove into the hardwood.

All eyes turned to me as I stepped into the room. Well, all but Callum's. He was deathly pale, his chest rising and falling so softly I could be forgiven for thinking he was dead.

"How...um, is Callum all right?" I worried at my bottom lip and forced myself to meet Reed's eyes. Had I hurt him by giving my energy? There was still so much to learn, and I had acted impulsively.

"He's fine, Little Spark, thanks to you."

Reed's gratitude cut off my self-recriminations. "Really?" Reed smiled and my breath left me in a rush. "Oh, thank God. I thought maybe I'd hurt him!"

I crossed the room and placed my hand on Callum's forehead. His skin was warm, and up close, I could see color returning to his cheeks. He seemed to be sleeping naturally.

"He said he was tiring and there were still zombies." I murmured as I watched the gentle rise and fall of his chest. "I didn't think about what transferring energy might do to a human."

Dante chuckled. "He's not human, and you saved him from weeks of recovery." I met his gaze, and he winked. "You did good, Lenox."

I blushed and managed a shaky smile. "I'm just glad I could help. You guys handled the tough parts."

A thoughtful silence settled over the room, broken only by the crackling fire. Derek stopped pacing and turned to Giles. "We need to figure out why zombies were attacking River Street," he said, voicing the question on everyone's mind.

Giles closed the tome with a thud and stood, his expression grave. "Indeed, Derek. We're dealing with a necromancer, someone who has bound spirits to do their bidding. This is dark magic of the highest order."

Reed whistled. "Necromancy!" He looked at Dante and then at Giles. "That explains the zombie horde, but why target River Street?"

Remembering the rotting corpses threatening people on the river walk made my skin crawl. I stepped closer to the fire, savoring its warmth for a moment before turning to address the room. "Why would a necromancer start an invasion on River Street? What was the purpose?"

Giles met my eyes, his voice steady but somber. "They were meant to capture you, Lenox."

My mouth dropped open. "Me! Why?"

Giles sighed deeply. "I suspect the ghost of Amelia Walsh has a tracking spell on her. The necromancer bound her spirit, and when you contacted her, it alerted him to your presence."

"So that's why Amelia came to warn me!" My stomach churned with nausea as I explained the ghost's appearance right before the attack. I should have heeded her. "I made myself a target by interacting with Amelia."

Giles nodded solemnly. "Yes, and it's even more complex than that. I deciphered the runes on the bones in the hex bag. They are written in an ancient language, one nearly forgotten. It was a spell to bind you to the necromancer, making you powerless to disobey him."

I swayed and, if not for Dante's quick reflexes, I'd have faceplanted on the floor.

"Easy, Lenox, we've got your back." He led me to the chair he'd occupied and then muttered something about getting me a glass of water.

Reed's eyes narrowed as he watched me for several seconds before turning back to Giles. "So, the necromancer wanted to control Lenox and use her abilities. That's seriously dangerous."

Dante scowled as he crossed the room, handing me a glass. "You're not kidding, Reed. We need to find this person fast."

He shared a dark look with Reed. "If someone like Lenox fell into the hands of a dark magic practitioner...they could conquer the world."

Reed let out a short laugh. "All of the worlds actually."

Someone like me? I was about to ask them what was so special about being able to talk to ghosts but Reed started peppering Giles with questions so I filed it away for a better time.

"I agree, Reed. We are dealing with a potentially realm-ending crisis but we've taken precautions. The property is protected and we are all carrying personal protection as well."

Reed huffed. "A lot of good that did Lenox tonight."

Giles pursed his lips. "Yes, but until a few hours ago, we didn't know the necromancer was aware of Lenox." He looked at me, his eyes serious. "From now on, you're not going anywhere alone, understood?"

I frowned, not thrilled about being babysat, but the look on Giles's face said not to argue. I bit back a sigh and nodded.

"Good. Now then, Reed. The necromancer has to be someone from the supernatural community or a very lucky human who somehow stumbled upon a grimoire or spell to reanimate the dead. Since you'd have better odds of hitting the lottery, I'm going with the supernatural connection. Can you think of anyone within your community that might be involved in dark magic?"

Reed rubbed his chin thoughtfully. "There have been a few expelled from the supernatural community for dabbling in forbidden magic or unethical behavior." He looked at Dante. "You think it's one of ours?"

He shrugged. "I hate to think so, but what Giles said makes sense. We've expelled a couple of people over the years that would fit the bill and, though I don't want to accuse anyone, I'd say it's better to be safe and check them out."

Reed sighed and tipped his head back to stare at the coffered ceiling. After a few moments of silence, he walked over to Giles's desk and started scribbling on a piece of paper. "Alaric, Maris, and Samuel." He looked at Dante. "Anyone I'm forgetting?"

Dante shrugged. "I'd add Garrick to the list."

Reed quirked a brow but dutifully wrote the name down.

Derek crossed to the desk and peered at the list Reed had made. "So who are these individuals and how can we find them?"

Reed explained. "Alaric is a fae. He was experimenting with old fae magic that was banned centuries ago. His intentions were to protect our community, but his illusions began to backfire."

Reed shook his head. "It was a mess. A group of college kids experienced one of his illusions in Forsyth Park and panicked, causing a small riot. That drew attention to our community, so we put it to the council and decided to expel him."

Derek nodded. "Council? There's a secret government as well as a tavern for non-humans?"

Reed laughed. "Yes, Detective, we've tried to replicate the system that was used in our home realm. By the way, not everyone within our community is from the supernatural realm. We do have magical humans among us."

Derek raised an eyebrow. "Interesting. So who else is on this list?"

"Maris. She's a witch who was experimenting with mind control spells. We deemed it too dangerous, and the council decided to expel her."

Derek tapped Reed's list. "And this Garrick? What did he do?"

"Aside from starting a brawl in the Twilight?" Dante chuckled. "Garrick is a werewolf, and they aren't known for having an even temper. As security for the club, I'd gotten used to his ways, but he crossed the line one night after Reed confronted him about dabbling in blood magic. He took exception to being questioned and went for Reed's throat. He was brought up on charges and the council suspended him. He's not outright banished, but a six-month ban until he completes therapy might as well be the same thing as I doubt he'll cooperate."

Derek's brows rose. "Violent and messes with blood magic? Sounds like he could be our guy. You know where we can locate him?"

Dante nodded. "His family has an old plantation in Georgetown. Reed should have the address in our files."

"Great." Derek looked down at the suspect list. "So that just leaves Samuel." He looked at Reed. "What did this guy do?"

Reed's expression darkened. "He fancies himself a scientist." He shook his head and huffed. "More like a mad scientist! He was conducting experiments on animals using arcane magic and pseudoscience. That was bad enough, but then we discovered he was using unwilling human subjects. The council had no choice but to boot him. His actions were an abomination, crossing every ethical boundary imaginable."

Giles cleared his throat, drawing everyone's attention. "Thank you, Reed, Dante. Tomorrow, we'll start our investigation with the names on this list." He glanced at the couch. "For now, let's check on Callum. He should have woken up by now. Maybe I should consult Selena—"

"I'm awake, sort of..." Callum mumbled, stretching with a jaw-cracking yawn."

We all crowded around, talking over each other as we asked how he was feeling and demanded he take it easy.

"Guys, one at a time!" He laughed and sat. "I'm fine, more than fine really, considering how much effort it takes to freeze humans in time and how long I held the spell."

Callum looked over at me. "I'd burned through my energy and was pulling from my life force. Without your unique essence, I might not have made it. You have my eternal gratitude."

I blinked, surprised. "You're welcome, glad I could help." I frowned as his words ran back through my mind. "You said unique essence. How can that be?"

Callum smiled gently. "I'm an elemental. Normally, a transfer like that from a human wouldn't have worked. Usually I can only draw energy from nature or another elemental. Your essence felt different, more powerful."

I frowned. "But I don't understand. I'm just an ordinary human, so why did it work?"

Reed chuckled softly. "Little Spark, you are far from ordinary. I suspect you aren't fully human, either."

18

QUESTIONABLE ORIGINS

The morning light streamed through the window, highlighting my face as I sat before the dressing table mirror. Dragging a brush through my hair, I stared at my reflection and tried to push the statement Reed had made last night from my mind.

I suspect you aren't fully human.

Not human? What had he meant by that? Catching my bottom lip between my teeth, I leaned closer to the mirror. Jet-black hair, light gray eyes, nose and lips in the normal places...of course I was human!

But Reed, Dante, and Callum all look human, the snide voice in my head reminded me. Wrinkling my nose at that uncomfortable truth, I swallowed past the lump in my throat and rose to get dressed.

Judging by some of the denizens frequenting the Twilight Tavern, looks could be deceiving when it came to the supernatural community. Could it be true? Was I like them?

My gaze drifted to the mirror as I considered the possibilities. Had Reed seen something in my aura, something that set me apart? Or was it just an observation based on my abilities?

I rolled my eyes and pulled a t-shirt over my head. The idea I was some other kind of being was silly. I'd been poked, prodded, and examined by medical professionals for almost a year without a hint I was abnormal. Reed had to have been teasing.

I managed to convince myself while dressing but catching sight of my reflection as I crossed the kitchen, my anxiety came roaring back.

There'd been something unsettling in Reed's eyes since the moment I'd met him; like he knew the punch line to a joke I hadn't even heard. I'd avoided thinking about it too closely but after his casually dropped bombshell... I sighed and made a cup of tea.

As I waited for the water to boil, my phone buzzed on the counter, startling me. I glanced at the screen and saw Julian's name flash. A brief smile tugged at my lips despite myself. I swiped to read his message.

Good morning! Care to join me for breakfast at that little bistro overlooking Madison Square? Promise I won't bore you with shop talk. Just good food and even better company.

I chuckled softly, but the smile faded as reality set in. Julian had been persistent, and I couldn't deny I was drawn to his charm. But with everything happening—the necromancer, the ghosts, Reed's cryptic warnings—there was no time for leisurely breakfasts with charming men.

I quickly typed back, *Would love to, but I'm swamped with work today. Rain check?* I hesitated before hitting send, hoping he wouldn't take it as a brush-off.

An immediate reply flashed across the screen, a single sad face emoji followed by, *You wound me! Depriving me of your company is cruel punishment indeed. But I'll take a rain check—just don't make me wait too long, or I might wither away from loneliness!*

I laughed, shaking my head. "Dramatic much?" I muttered to myself, a small smile lingering despite the chaos of the day ahead.

The kettle whistled, pulling me from my thoughts. I poured the water over the teabag, watching the dark color spread, and felt a pang of guilt for dodging Julian again. Maybe once things settled down...

A knock at the door and a request I hurry out to the driveway shook me from my reverie and reminded me that I had more pressing concerns.

Focus, Lenox, I muttered to myself. Today, we would start interviewing the suspects Reed and Dante had provided and, with the very real and increasingly personal danger the necromancer posed, my head needed to be in the game.

Draining my mug of tea with a big gulp, I grabbed my keys and headed out to meet Giles, but the thought lingered—there was more to my story, something crucial from my past that needed to be uncovered, and Reed was the place to start.

Staring blindly out the window as Derek drove to Alaric's, I contemplated what we were about to do. I fingered the black tourmaline protection stone dangling from my neck and prayed it would be enough to keep me safe. Despite Giles's assurances, I still wasn't convinced we should attempt confronting a supernatural being without one of them on our side.

Giles turned to me from the passenger seat, his voice measured but firm. "Remember, I'm going to ask the questions while Derek observes his body language. We'll be distracted, so your job is to be alert for any use of magic. Let me know if you sense anything unusual, all right?"

Swallowing hard, I nodded and let his lessons about magical signatures run through my mind—each spell had a distinctive fingerprint, from a skin-tingling sensation to subtle changes in the air. I had to stay alert, ready to sense anything out of the ordinary.

Derek slowed the car and pulled into the nature pre-serve, shaking me from my reverie. Leaning forward, I looked through the windshield. "Why are we stopping here?"

Giles released his seatbelt as Derek cut the engine. "This is where Alaric lives." He exited the car, leaning down to speak before shutting the door. "From here, we walk."

Waving for us to follow, Giles crossed the parking lot and quickly disappeared down a tree-lined path. My brows shot up and, after exchanging a look with Derek, we jogged to catch up.

As we fell into step behind Giles, the cool, damp air of the forest surrounded us, the leaves crunching under our feet. I could sense something was on Derek's mind, his usual easygoing demeanor replaced by a noticeable tension.

He cleared his throat, looking uncomfortable as we set-tled into a steady pace. "I visited my parents the other night," he began, his voice low. "I told them about Emily."

A pang of sympathy washed over me, and I reached out to place a hand on his arm in consolation. "Derek, I'm so sorry. That must have been incredibly hard."

He nodded, his eyes downcast. But before I could say more, I caught myself and asked, "Wait...you told your parents I talk to ghosts?"

Derek glanced at me, a faint smirk pulling at the corners of his mouth. "Yeah, I did. There was no other way to tell them she's gone."

My breath caught in my throat as I imagined how that conversation must have gone. Before I could respond, Derek sighed deeply, the sound weighted with years of buried grief.

"They were inconsolable. I guess I should have expected it, but it's been almost twenty years since she went missing. How could they still have hope she was alive?"

"Sometimes," I said softly, "faith and hope are all that keep us going."

Derek exhaled roughly, his frustration palpable. "Yeah. I guess I've just become cynical."

He kicked at a loose stone on the path, sending it skittering into the underbrush, then turned to me, his expression serious. "Fallout from telling them is that I need to ask a big favor."

I blinked in surprise. "Of course, anything I can do."

He slowed his pace slightly, turning to face me fully. "I need you to come with me to visit my parents. I want you to try to talk to Emily."

I sucked in a breath, taken aback by the request. My mind raced with the implications, and I could feel the weight of what he was asking settle heavily on my shoulders. "I can do that, Derek, but...are you sure that's a good idea?"

He let out a tired chuckle, more weary than amused. "No, but they want to talk to her, and if I'm honest...so do I." He ran a hand through his hair, the tension in his body evident. "The diary I found?"

I nodded, urging him to continue.

"Emily wrote about a friend who gave her a necklace and told her it was their secret." His voice hardened, and his eyes locked onto mine, filled with a determined resolve. "Her keepsake box had a necklace, Lenox. I took it to Park Jewelers. It's a real diamond pendant, twenty-four karat gold. No kid is able to give a friend something like that."

I frowned, the significance of his words sinking in. "Gosh, I wouldn't think so, but is that significant to what happened to Emily?"

He nodded, his voice clipped and edged with anger. "Pedophiles groom their victims by gifting them things, making them feel special, telling them it's their secret. I hope I'm wrong, but..." His voice faltered for a moment, the emotion breaking through. "Mom and Dad want to know where her body is, but I want to know how she died and who her 'friend' was."

A wave of sadness washed over me as I processed what he was saying. My throat tightened and I licked my lips, searching for the right words. "Derek, I'm so sorry. I can't imagine how hard this must be for you. I'll do whatever I can, but don't get your hopes up too high. Ghosts...they're not always clear about what happened to them. Remember when Amelia asked for my help and told me the angels sang her to sleep? Emily might be even less aware of what happened to her."

Derek nodded, though the determination in his eyes didn't waver. "I get it, but I have to try. I need to know."

"I understand," I said softly, squeezing his arm in reassurance. "I'll help you, Derek. We'll do everything we can to find out the truth."

The weight of his grief lingered between us. I was about to offer more comfort when something caught Derek's attention. He squinted, his expression shifting from serious to bewildered. "Uh... is Giles okay?"

I followed his gaze and nearly stopped in my tracks. Up ahead in an open field Giles was making strange gestures with his hands, almost like he was conducting an invisible orchestra, his mouth moving rapidly as he talked to...nothing.

"Giles?" I called out, half-concerned, half-amused. "Are you... talking to the air?"

He didn't respond immediately, too engrossed in whatever ritual he was performing. I glanced at Derek, who looked equally perplexed. Just as I was about to call out to him again, there was a sudden flash of light, and the air seemed to shimmer.

Before our eyes, the outline of a quaint little cottage began to materialize, its stone walls covered in ivy, smoke lazily drifting from the chimney.

Giles turned back to us with a satisfied grin. "Welcome to Alaric's humble abode," he said, as if nothing unusual had happened.

I exchanged a wide-eyed look with Derek.

He shook his head in disbelief. "I'm never getting used to this kind of thing."

Grinning, I followed Giles to the front door. He knocked three times, the sound echoing through the silent field. A moment later, the door creaked open, revealing a tall, thin man with sharp features and piercing eyes—Alaric.

"Giles," Alaric greeted, his voice laced with both irritation and curiosity, like honeyed wine that had soured. "To what do I owe this unexpected visit?"

"Alaric," Giles replied, his tone suddenly serious but polite, almost cautious. "We need to talk."

Alaric's eyes flicked to Derek and me, his gaze lingering on me a moment longer than was comfortable. His lips curled slightly, more a sneer than a smile. "You brought friends. How charming. Well, you might as well come in, then."

He begrudgingly stepped aside, and we followed him into the cottage. The interior was as cozy as its exterior suggested—wooden beams, a small fireplace crackling in the corner, and shelves lined with books and strange artifacts. Despite the warmth, an underlying tension crackled in the air.

Giles took a seat without waiting for an invitation, his expression thoughtful. "I have to admit, Alaric, it's been a while. How have you been keeping yourself?"

Alaric leaned against the mantel, crossing his arms over his chest. "Oh, you know, keeping busy. Research, the occasional spell work. Nothing out of the ordinary. Why?"

Giles leaned back, his posture relaxed but his eyes sharp. "Just curious. It's not often I hear your name mentioned these days. In fact, the last time was...well, yesterday."

Alaric's gaze narrowed slightly, but he kept his tone light, though edged with sarcasm. "You don't say. And what was the occasion? A gathering of old friends? Rude that you didn't invite me."

Giles chuckled softly. "No, nothing quite so formal. Just an interesting event downtown. A zombie attack, actually. Very unusual for Savannah."

Alaric's expression didn't change, but I noticed a slight tightening around his eyes. "Zombies, you say? How dreadful. And you think I had something to do with this?"

Giles shrugged nonchalantly. "Well, it's certainly not the sort of thing one expects to happen in broad daylight. Or even at night, for that matter. But you have a reputation for...unconventional practices."

Alaric's lips thinned into a tight line. "Unconventional does not equate to illegal or malicious, Giles. You of all people should know that."

Derek stepped forward, his stance tense, eyes fixed on Alaric. "Where were you last night, Alaric?"

Alaric's gaze flicked to Derek, a flicker of annoyance crossing his features. "Not that it's any of your business, but I was here, alone. Reading." He uncrossed his arms and gestured to a pile of books on a nearby table. "I'm a bit of a night owl, you know."

Giles nodded slowly, as if considering his next words carefully. "And during your, uh, nocturnal studies, you didn't happen to, I don't know, notice anything unusual? Any strange energies, perhaps?"

Alaric's patience seemed to fray a bit more. He straightened up, his tone more clipped. "What exactly are you getting at, Giles?"

Giles's expression turned serious, losing its earlier lightness. "Reed mentioned you've been working on a spell that was banned—a powerful illusion spell, if I'm not mistaken. We're just trying to understand if there's any connection to what happened last night."

Alaric bristled at the mention of Reed's name, his eyes flashing with irritation. "Reed has always had a loose tongue. Yes, I've dabbled in a spell that could be considered forbidden, by some—strictly for research purposes, mind you. It's not dark magic. I was merely trying to understand its mechanics. There's a difference."

Derek folded his arms, clearly unimpressed. "A difference that involves raising the dead?"

Alaric's face flushed with indignation. "I have no interest in raising the dead." He scowled. "And who are you to pry into my affairs?"

Derek started to answer, but Giles beat him to it. "Where are my manners?" He gestured toward Derek and me. "This is Detective Derek Vance of the Savannah Police Department, and Lenox Grady works for me."

Alaric's face flushed scarlet. "How dare you bring human law enforcement to my home!" Fists clenched, he began to stalk around the small room. "I trusted you with the spell to enter my property and this is how you repay a friend?" His gaze swung to me. "And that abomination works for you?" He spat out the words and sneered at Giles. "What kind of a game are you playing?"

Abomination? I bristled, a surge of anger flaring up inside me. It was clear he looked down on humans, and I wasn't about to let this bigotry go unchallenged. I opened my mouth, ready to fire back, but caught Giles's almost imperceptible shake of his head. I clenched my teeth, swallowing my retort, the insult still burning hot.

Alaric continued, his voice still laced with venom. "I resent even the implication I might practice necromancy! That kind of power is dangerous, and I know better than to meddle in such matters. I was studying containment, not conjuration."

Giles tilted his head, studying Alaric's reaction closely. "Research, yes...but you can see why we might be concerned, given the timing and the nature of the incident."

Alaric's eyes narrowed. "I see where this is going. You think I had something to do with the zombies. I assure you, Giles, if I wanted to stir up trouble, I'd choose a more...sophisticated method."

Giles smiled faintly, though it didn't reach his eyes. He leaned forward, his tone still measured but firm. "Sophisticated or not, we have to follow every lead. Perhaps you could suggest someone else who might be less...discerning in their practices?"

Alaric's irritation flared, a spark of annoyance flickering in his eyes. He folded his arms tighter across his chest, his lips curling into a sneer. "You think I keep a list of every miscreant in Savannah? I have no idea who's meddling with the undead, and frankly, I don't care. My research is my own, Giles. I don't concern myself with the affairs of the city's less savory characters."

He paused, his gaze shifting between the three of us, as if deciding whether to say more. "You come barging in here, making accusations, disturbing my peace..." His voice lowered, almost a growl. "It's a wonder I've tolerated this intrusion for as long as I have."

Alaric took a step closer to Giles, his eyes narrowing, the sneer deepening into something more menacing. "Now go, all of you," he finally snapped, his voice cold and cutting. "Before I decide to make your visit far more memorable."

As Alaric issued his not-so-subtle threat, the air in the room grew heavier, almost suffocating. A sharp, metallic taste coated my tongue, like copper or blood, making me grimace.

My skin prickled, a sense of danger settling over me like a shadow. It wasn't overwhelming, but it lingered—like a faint whisper of something lurking just out of sight. I clasped my protective pendant, feeling its warmth against my palm, and met Giles's gaze. His expression hardened, his eyes sharp and unyielding.

"Easy now, Alaric," Giles said, his voice calm but with an edge that suggested he wasn't to be trifled with. "We're not here to cause trouble, and I'd hate to see things escalate unnecessarily. We're leaving now. No need for theatrics." He paused for a beat, his gaze never wavering. "But remember—if anything happens to us on the way out, there will be consequences."

Alaric's eyes flickered with a dangerous glint, but he remained silent, his lips pressed into a thin line. Unspoken threats hung between us. As we turned to leave, my heart thudded in my chest, tension coiling in my gut. My grip tightened on the pendant at my neck, its warmth a small comfort against the cold fear coursing through me.

Outside, the path back to the car seemed longer than before, each rustling leaf and snapping twig making my pulse jump. I glanced at Derek, his eyes scanning the shadows, his posture tense and ready. Giles walked ahead, his shoulders set with determination, but I could see the tightness in his jaw.

A chill ran down my spine as I thought about the other suspects we still had to interview. If Alaric was willing to issue a veiled threat, who knew what the others might do when cornered?

I swallowed hard, forcing myself to stay focused. One thing was clear—this wasn't going to get any easier. The real danger might still be ahead, lurking in the shadows of our next encounter.

As we reached the car, I cast one last glance back toward Alaric's hidden cottage. Whatever lay ahead, I had to be ready for anything. And I had the sinking feeling that this was just the beginning.

19
WHISPERED WARNINGS

As we pulled away from Alaric's hidden cottage, his words clung to me like the damp mist swirling around the trees. *Abomination.* The label had settled deep in my chest, heavy and unnerving, making it hard to focus on anything else.

I stared out the window, watching the shadows of the forest slide past. The world outside seemed unchanged, peaceful even, but inside, my thoughts churned like a storm.

Abomination. What did he see in me? What did they all see?

The question nagged at me, growing louder with every passing mile. My reflection in the glass looked the same—same black hair, same gray eyes—but Alaric's words wouldn't let me dismiss the idea that something was wrong.

And Reed...Reed had *known,* hadn't he? He had looked at me like I was some*thing* to figure out, not some*one.*

I pressed my forehead against the cool window and closed my eyes, trying to steady the whirlwind inside.

I suspect you aren't fully human.

Reed's words echoed in my mind. Was it true? Was that why I could see and talk to ghosts? Why I could transfer energy like I had with Callum? It had always felt like a gift, but now I wasn't sure. If I wasn't human, then what was I?

I stole a glance at Giles, hoping for some kind of reassurance, but his face was unreadable as always, eyes focused on the road ahead. Did he know more than he was letting on? Was that why he'd taken me in so easily? The thought made my stomach twist.

I'm not an abomination, I told myself, gripping the black tourmaline pendant around my neck. But the doubt lingered, gnawing at the edges of my mind. If even Reed and Alaric could see something different in me, how long would it be before Derek or Julian saw it too? Would they look at me like some kind of...thing?

The silence in the car stretched on, thick and suffocating, and I felt the weight of Alaric's insult pressing down on me. I had no memories, no past to guide me. What if there was something buried in those missing years that I didn't want to uncover?

I clenched my fists, anger flaring up to meet the fear. I wasn't going to let them define me. Not Alaric, not Reed, not anyone. If there was something more to me, something lurking beneath the surface, then I'd find it out myself—on *my* terms. But I wasn't going to let them dictate who I was.

I wasn't just an abomination.

I was Lenox Grady. And I'd figure this out. One way or another.

But even as I tried to hold onto that stubborn resolve, doubt still curled in the pit of my stomach. How could I figure out something that seemed buried so deep inside me, when I didn't even know where to start? The questions wouldn't stop circling in my mind, refusing to leave me alone. Maybe I did need help—at least to understand what I was up against.

Taking a deep breath, I swallowed my pride.

"Giles," I said quietly, breaking the silence. My voice sounded smaller than I'd intended. "What did Alaric mean by calling me an abomination?"

Giles turned toward me, his eyes thoughtful, though his expression remained serious. "It's an outdated term," he said, his voice measured. "In the supernatural community, there are those who see any mixing of species—whether human or supernatural—as unnatural. To them, such beings are considered abominations."

The word hit me harder than it had the first time. My breath hitched. "So...Alaric thinks I'm some kind of half-breed?"

Giles sighed softly. "Alaric is an old soul. His views are from another time. What he thinks doesn't define you, Lenox. You are who you are—no matter what anyone else might say."

But was I? Did I even know who I really was?

I nodded, pretending to accept Giles's reassurance, but the knot in my stomach only tightened. I wasn't so sure anymore. "And Reed?" I asked, remembering the fae's piercing gaze, the way he looked at me as if he could see something hidden just beneath my skin. "Does he think the same?"

Giles hesitated, and for a moment, I thought he might not answer. But then he spoke, his voice quieter. "Reed is...*curious*. He sees things others don't. I suspect he's trying to figure you out, just as we all are."

A lump rose in my throat. If even Giles had doubts about what I was, what hope did I have of understanding myself? I wanted to press further, to ask more questions, but something in Giles's tone told me this wasn't the time. Not yet.

Derek shifted in his seat, breaking the tension. "We're almost there," he said, nodding toward a break in the trees ahead. "Jericho River is dead ahead. Which way do I turn at the stop sign?"

I turned my attention to the landscape outside. The trees began to thin, giving way to patches of dense undergrowth and swampy terrain. I could see flashes of water through the gaps, the river winding its way through the lowlands. The air seemed to change, growing heavier with an almost palpable sense of foreboding.

"Remember," Giles said, his tone turning authoritative again, "Maris is fiercely protective of her coven. She doesn't trust easily, especially not after everything they've been through with the developers and the government. She might see us as another threat, so we need to be careful how we approach this."

Derek nodded, his eyes narrowing with determination. "Understood. We're here to gather information, not to provoke her."

The road narrowed to a dirt path, the car jolting over ruts and roots. Overhanging live oaks formed a canopy that blocked the sun, the scent of damp earth filling the air. The forest seemed to close in, watching. Ahead, the trees parted, revealing a shadowy fence, barely visible in the gloom.

We rounded a bend, and a gate appeared between two ancient oaks. The iron bars were twisted and gnarled, like skeletal fingers reaching out to grab us. A figure stood in front, wrapped in a dark cloak, her face hidden in the shadows.

Derek brought the car to a stop as Giles rolled down his window. "Maris," he called out, his tone even but firm. "We're here to talk. We mean no harm."

The figure shifted, and for a moment, I thought she might simply turn us away. But then she stepped forward, the hood of her cloak falling back to reveal a stern, weathered face framed by wild, gray-streaked hair.

"You have a strange way of showing it, Giles," she replied, her voice rough, like gravel underfoot. "Bringing outsiders to my door." She leaned over and peered through the window, her steel gray eyes landing first on Derek, whom she dismissed with a disdainful sniff and a toss of her head, then to me.

Her gaze roamed over me for several taut seconds, making my skin crawl. She inhaled through her nose and then her eyes widened. Maris backed away from the window and fixed Giles with a furious glare. "You bring a human and a rogue into my territory?"

The hostility in her tone made me clutch at my pendant. A rogue? First, I'm an abomination, and now I'm a rogue. What did that even mean? Did everyone in the supernatural world know something about me that I didn't?

My face flushed with anger and a twinge of fear. I wanted to snap back, to challenge her right then and there, but I bit my tongue, forcing myself to stay silent. Giles had warned us not to provoke her, but if they expected me to cower in fear, they were mistaken. I might not understand what they saw in me, but I wasn't about to let their labels define me.

Keep it together, I told myself.

But doubt gnawed at the edges of my mind. Maris's eyes were sharp, like she could see something lurking beneath the surface that even I couldn't grasp. For so long, I'd feared what might be out there, in the shadows. But now, a more terrifying thought crept in: What if I was the one to be feared?

We were seated around a low, smoldering fire pit—well, Giles and Derek were. Since I was apparently a "rogue," whatever that meant, the witches insisted I sit a few feet away inside a small protection circle. The circle was drawn hastily with chalk on the ground, the lines glowing faintly with a soft blue light. It felt more like a cage than a precaution, as though I were a dangerous animal under observation.

As I settled into the circle, the faint hum of the containment spell buzzed around me and the atmosphere seemed to grow heavier. The damp earth beneath me was cold and unforgiving, sending a deep, penetrating chill through my bones.

The air was thick with the scent of wet leaves and burning herbs. Shadows danced across the ground, cast by the flickering flames. I could feel the witches' eyes on me, their whispers filled with both fear and curiosity.

My hands tightened around the black tourmaline pendant at my neck, the familiar weight a small comfort against the unsettling sense of confinement. The forest around us seemed to hold its breath, waiting.

I stole a glance at Giles, who seemed outwardly calm, though I could tell he was on high alert. His eyes were sharp, watching Maris with the intensity of a hawk observing its prey. Maris herself sat across from us, her posture relaxed, but there was a coiled tension in the set of her shoulders, a slyness in her smile that suggested she was waiting for the right moment to pounce.

She leaned back in her chair, her gaze drifting between the three of us, finally settling on Giles. "So, Giles," she began, her voice smooth as silk but carrying an edge. "What exactly brings you and your...companions to my doorstep today? I'm sure it's not for a friendly chat."

Giles offered a small, diplomatic smile. "We're investigating a series of disturbances in the city," he replied evenly. "Unnatural occurrences. You've likely heard of the recent zombie attack?"

Maris's expression didn't change, but I saw a flicker of something in her eyes—interest, perhaps, or maybe amusement. "Oh, yes, I've heard whispers. But Savannah is always full of such gossip. Ghosts, ghouls, zombies... Is that not your area of expertise?"

Giles's smile didn't waver. "It is, which is why we're here. There are rumors of certain spells—dark spells—being cast in this area. We thought it prudent to ask a few questions."

Maris chuckled, a low, throaty sound that made my stomach clench. "Dark spells, you say?" She leaned forward slightly, her eyes gleaming with a predatory light. "And you assume, what, that I'm involved because I'm a witch? Or perhaps because I have a vested interest in keeping my coven and our land safe?"

Derek spoke up, his tone measured but firm. "We're not here to make accusations, Maris. We just want to understand what's going on. Protecting your coven is one thing, but if it involves dark magic—"

Maris cut him off with a sharp wave of her hand. "Save your breath, Detective," she snapped, her tone suddenly cold. "You have no authority here, and neither does the city." Her gaze flicked back to Giles, her expression softening just a fraction. "But you, Giles...you should know better than to come here with such suspicions. Especially after all we've been through."

Giles leaned forward slightly, his eyes narrowing. "I'm here because of what we've been through, Maris. I know you're protective of your coven and your land, and I respect that. But there are lines that shouldn't be crossed. Lines that endanger more than just your enemies."

Maris's smile faded, replaced by a look of irritation. "I don't need a lecture on ethics, Giles," she retorted. "I'm well aware of the risks and the costs. But you come here, bringing outsiders and"—she glanced at me, her nose wrinkling slightly—"other...elements, and expect me to just spill all my secrets?"

Giles maintained his calm demeanor, though I could see a muscle in his jaw twitching. "I'm not asking for your secrets, Maris. Just your cooperation. If you know anything about the recent events—anything at all—it could help prevent further harm. That's all we're trying to do."

Maris studied him for a long moment, her gaze unreadable. Finally, she sighed and leaned back, crossing her arms over her chest. "You always were persistent," she muttered. "Fine. I'll tell you what I know, but don't expect much. And understand this—I'm doing this out of respect for you, not for them." She nodded toward Derek and me, her expression hardening again.

Giles nodded in acknowledgment. "Thank you, Maris. That's all we ask."

Maris's eyes flicked around the circle, as if deciding how much to reveal. The fire crackled between us, casting haunting shadows across her face. "There's been...strange activity," she began slowly, her voice lowering to a near whisper. "Dark rituals on some of the deserted islands near our coven's land. They disturb even the most seasoned among us."

Giles leaned forward, his attention sharp. "Rituals? What kind of rituals?"

Maris hesitated, her gaze sliding over to me for a brief second before focusing back on Giles. "Rituals with a purpose. Older, darker magic—the kind that stirs the wind and whispers to the shadows. We found sigils that seemed to pulse, bones arranged in patterns, stones marked with otherworldly glyphs. It's as if...someone or something is trying to tear open the fabric between worlds, to break a barrier meant to remain closed."

Giles's eyes narrowed. "A door to where?"

Maris's expression darkened, her lips tightening. A flicker of fear—or perhaps frustration—crossed her features, gone as quickly as it appeared. "To the supernatural realm, perhaps. Or beyond..." She paused, her voice dropping to a near whisper, as if afraid the very shadows around us might hear. "The energies at play were not just for raising the dead—they're pulling at something deeper, something that lies in wait."

A chill ran down my spine. The implications of what she was saying were terrifying. "And these symbols...they're for opening a portal?" I asked, trying to keep my voice steady.

Maris nodded grimly. "Yes. Whoever it is, they're trying to tear open a gateway. To what end, I can't say. But it's not just about controlling the undead. They're seeking a passage, a way to breach the realms."

Giles's face darkened. "A portal to the supernatural realm...or worse. And these rituals, they align with the recent zombie attacks?"

Maris nodded slowly. "The timing is too close to be a coincidence. The energies being manipulated—they're not just for raising the dead. It's bigger than that. They're reaching for something...someone."

Derek, who had been silent until now, spoke up. "Do you know who's behind these rituals?"

Maris shook her head. "No. But the power involved...it's not the work of a single witch or warlock. This is orchestrated. Someone with a deep knowledge of necromancy, someone willing to risk everything for what they want."

Giles seemed to be deep in thought, his brows furrowing. "If they succeed in opening a portal, it could bring chaos. Not just to Savannah but to both worlds."

Maris's gaze flicked to Derek, her expression unreadable. "I don't know who it is. But if I were you, I'd be preparing for a war. They're not just stirring up the dead—they're preparing for something much larger. A convergence."

Giles's eyes sharpened at the word. "A convergence? Of what?"

Maris shrugged. "Of realms? Of powers? I can't say, but if they manage to open that door, you'd better be ready for whatever comes through."

I could feel her gaze on me again, and my skin crawled under her scrutiny. "Why are you even helping them, Giles?" she asked suddenly, her voice sharp. "This isn't your fight."

Giles held her gaze steadily. "If dark forces are at play, it becomes all our fight, Maris. You know that."

A sneer curled her thin lips as her gaze fell on me and then Derek. "Humans have done nothing but harm to our community, I owe them nothing. My responsibility is to my coven. I have to protect them, and I'll do whatever it takes to ensure their safety."

Giles gave a small nod, his expression understanding yet firm. "I wouldn't expect anything less from you, Maris. But remember—if this threat grows, it won't stop at your borders. It will come for all of us."

Her eyes remained steely, her posture defiant, but I noticed a flicker of something else in her expression—doubt, perhaps, or fear. She swallowed tightly, her gaze briefly shifting to the witches around her, their eyes reflecting both uncertainty and trust in their leader. Maris's shoulders stiffened, as if she were steeling herself against some invisible force.

She let out a slow, measured breath, the tension in her body easing just a fraction. "You're right," she admitted reluctantly, her voice softer but still edged with steel. "But make no mistake, Giles—I will not risk my coven's safety for the likes of them." She shot another glance at Derek and me, her eyes narrowing. "And don't expect me to stand idle if things get out of hand," she added, her gaze returning to Giles, a steely resolve in her eyes. "I won't hesitate to protect what's mine."

Her words lingered in the air, laden with warning, but beneath her defiance, I sensed a begrudging acknowledgment of the shared danger we faced. The firelight flickered over her face, casting shadows that seemed to deepen the lines of worry etched into her features.

For a brief moment, the hardness in her eyes softened, revealing a glimpse of the fear that lay beneath her bravado. Then, just as quickly, her mask of steely resolve slipped back into place.

Giles inclined his head. "I understand. And thank you. We appreciate your cooperation."

Maris gave a curt nod, her expression still guarded. "Don't mistake this for friendship, Giles. I told you what I know out of respect for our past, not out of kindness." She glanced at Derek and me, her gaze full of suspicion and disdain. "And make sure *they* understand that."

Maris stood, signaling the end of the conversation. "You should go now," she said curtly. "Before my patience runs out."

We stood as well, tension building in my shoulders as we made our way back to the car. The witches around us continued to whisper and cast furtive glances our way, their eyes lingering on me with both curiosity and contempt. I kept my head high, my grip tightening on the pendant around my neck, and tried to ignore the uneasy feeling gnawing at my stomach.

We had just opened the gate when Maris's voice cut through the chilly air one last time, stopping us in our tracks.

"Giles," she called out, her tone suddenly softer but laced with something that made my skin crawl—a note of genuine concern, perhaps? "A word of warning."

We paused, looking back at her.

"Those who toy with the dead are mere apprentices to what's really coming," Maris whispered, her eyes unfocused. "What you saw on River Street...it's only the symptom, nothing more. There's a force behind it—older than necromancy, older than any of us. It's watching, waiting, and it's cold. So very cold."

Her voice faltered for just a moment, and the firelight seemed to dim, as if her words had stolen the warmth from the air. "Whatever you think you're fighting...it's much bigger than you."

As Maris spoke, the air around us seemed to thicken, the shadows stretching and twisting, almost as if reacting to her words. Her gaze was distant, like she was peering into a future only she could see.

"The undead rise, but they are not the end; they are the beginning. Mark my words, there's someone—something—pulling strings, setting pieces in motion. And every death, every ritual, is a step closer to breaking through. Whatever is happening, it's far from over."

Her words lingered in the air, sending a shiver down my spine. Her warning pressed on me, like a cold hand clutching at my heart.

Giles nodded slowly, his expression somber. "I understand, Maris. Thank you for the warning."

Dread crawled up my spine, Maris's words hanging like a dark omen. I glanced at Giles for reassurance, but his unreadable expression only deepened my unease. Whatever was coming, it was far more dangerous than we'd imagined—and time was running out.

20

GHOSTLY OMENS

The tour was nearly over, and we stood in Madison Square, surrounded by the sprawling oaks draped with Spanish moss. The square, usually serene, felt different tonight. The air was thick with humidity, and beneath the sharp scent of jasmine was a sense of heaviness—an unspoken warning that hung in the air like the moss itself.

I moved through my usual routine, weaving tales of the haunted history surrounding the square. My voice, usually animated and steady, wavered slightly as I found my gaze continuously drawn to the corner of the square—toward the looming oak tree that stood shrouded in shadow. And there, standing beneath its canopy, was him.

The weeping soldier.

His figure was barely more than a silhouette, blending into the darkness with an ethereal shimmer. I had seen him once before during another tour, but tonight, his presence felt more urgent. Like he was waiting for me.

I pushed through the last part of the tour, urging the group to explore while I gathered myself. The tourists dispersed, taking pictures, and I walked slowly toward the soldier, my heart beating a little faster with each step.

His eyes, hollow and filled with sorrow, locked onto mine as I approached. He didn't move, but his presence seemed to expand, like the air around him was pulsing with energy. "You see me," he said, his voice little more than a whisper, his words barely louder than the wind rustling through the moss.

I nodded, the chill in the air deepening. "Yes. I see you. What's wrong?"

His form flickered, and for a moment, I thought he might fade away. But then his gaze sharpened, filled with a sudden intensity. "The fires...will rise again..."

A cold dread shot through me. "What fires? What are you talking about?"

His eyes widened, and his voice turned hoarse, like he was struggling to speak against some unseen force. "He rises...the gates...will fall...the world will burn."

The weight of his words crushed against me, a warning thick with danger. "Who rises? What gates? You need to tell me more."

But the soldier's ghostly form began to waver, like smoke caught in a gust of wind. His mouth moved, but the words barely escaped. "Darkness...comes..."

And then he was gone. His spectral figure dissolved into the night, leaving me standing in the empty square with only the suffocating sense of dread lingering in the air.

My hands trembled as I clutched the pendant around my neck. Whatever this meant, it was clear that things were escalating. The necromancer, the gates, the fires—everything was converging toward something far worse than I had anticipated.

I needed to find Giles. Whatever the soldier's warning meant, we had to figure it out. Fast.

21

SHADOW HISTORY

The weeping soldier's message replayed in my mind on an endless loop as I finished the tour by rote. My words were automatic, my thoughts elsewhere, tangled in the ghost's cryptic warning.

Once free from my obligations, I rushed across Monterey Square to the Westlake Mansion, breathless and uneasy. I hadn't even finished recounting what the ghost had said before Giles's expression darkened, his eyes narrowing with both recognition and alarm.

The warning had made little sense to me, but after only a few moments of consideration, Giles had insisted we needed to consult with Reed. Whatever it was, it had struck a nerve with him—enough to put us on high alert. And now, here we were, rushing through the winding streets of Savannah toward the Twilight Tavern.

My footsteps echoed against the cobblestones, each step quick and purposeful. "What do you think the ghost meant, Giles?" I asked, glancing over at him as we made our way through a shadowed alley.

He shook his head, his expression grim. "I have some ideas, but I don't want to jump to conclusions. If anyone can confirm what the ghost's words meant, it's Reed."

I nodded, my mind racing. The ghost's words carried an urgency I couldn't quite grasp. What fires? What gates? And how did it all tie into Amelia's murder? The questions swirled as we entered the Clusky tombs.

Giles pulled his medallion from his pocket and pressed it against a worn brick in the wall. With a soft rumble, a section of the wall slid open, revealing the narrow alley that led to the tavern. We stepped through, and in seconds, we were standing under the dim lighting of the Twilight Tavern.

The pub was alive with activity, a cacophony of sounds and sights that could only belong to the supernatural world. Shapeshifters lounged in shadowed corners, their eyes gleaming with a strange inner light as they conversed in hushed tones.

A group of fae danced near the center of the room, their laughter like chimes, light and melodic, creating an enchanting backdrop to the otherwise chaotic scene. A trio of vampires huddled over drinks at the bar, their eyes flickering to new arrivals, equal parts suspicion and curiosity.

The scent of magic filled the room—a heady mix of earthy musk and sharp ozone—accompanied by the hum of lively music from an unseen band.

Dante spotted us from across the room. His gaze sharpened as he took in Giles's grim expression, and he quickly made his way over. "Giles, Lenox," he greeted, his voice low and smooth, but I detected a hint of concern beneath his casual demeanor. "What brings you here?"

"We need to see Reed," Giles said, his tone leaving no room for argument. "Now."

Dante's eyes flicked between us, sensing the urgency. "Alright, follow me," he said, leading us through the crowded room. I glanced around, taking in more of the patrons—werewolves, warlocks, beings I couldn't even name—all engrossed in their own conversations, oblivious to the storm brewing.

Dante led us down a short hallway to a sturdy wooden door. He knocked twice before pushing it open, revealing a cozy office lined with old books and relics that looked ancient and otherworldly.

Reed looked up from behind his desk, his dark eyes narrowing as he saw us. "Giles," he said, a hint of surprise in his voice. "What's going on?"

Giles wasted no time. "We've had more developments. Maris warned us of dark forces aligning and spoke of a resurgence in ancient, dangerous magic. And tonight, an old soldier ghost appeared to Lenox with a message, something about fires rising, gates falling...the world burning."

Reed's face paled slightly as he processed Giles's words. "Are you suggesting this is connected to the Shadowveil War in Aetheria? Or its aftermath?"

Giles nodded, his expression tense. "It's beginning to look that way. Maris's warning was vague, but the soldier's words were too specific, too similar to the events from the Shadowveil War."

Reed shook his head, his skepticism evident. "The Shadowveil War was centuries ago, Giles. We closed those gates for a reason, to prevent something like that from ever happening again. You really think this necromancer has the power to break those seals?"

Dante interjected, his tone measured. "Think about it, Reed. Why would a ghost—one who's been silent for so long—suddenly appear with a warning now, talking about fires and gates? What could have stirred it?"

Reed hesitated, dragging a hand through his hair—a rare display of unease. "Alright. Let's say you're right. If this is tied to the Shadowveil War, then we're dealing with something far worse than a rogue necromancer." He sighed and paced the room. "This is bad..."

Dante snorted. "Master of the understatement, my friend. This is bad with a capital B."

I watched their exchange, frustration bubbling up inside me. They seemed to be talking in circles, using terms and references I couldn't fully grasp. Finally, I huffed, crossing my arms. "Will someone please tell me what all this means?"

Reed's gaze shifted to me, a hint of a smirk breaking through his seriousness. "My apologies, Little Spark." He motioned to a leather winged-back chair across from his desk. "Have a seat. Time for a little history lesson."

Reed leaned back in his chair, his expression turning serious again. "So you see, Lenox, if we're correctly interpreting your ghost's warnings, this business with the necromancer could be linked to the events of the Shadowveil Wars in Aetheria."

I frowned, trying to make sense of it all. "And Aetheria is...your home?"

Reed nodded. "That's right. Aetheria is what humans refer to as the supernatural realm. It's a world where magic is interwoven with every aspect of life. But it's also a place marked by endless conflict, power struggles, and ancient grudges, especially during the Shadowveil Wars."

"I can see why you left," I murmured.

Reed chuckled, a knowing smile playing at his lips as he exchanged a brief glance with Dante, a silent understanding passing between them. "It certainly factored into the decision."

The shared look between them suggested there was more to Reed's departure from Aetheria than he was letting on, but now wasn't the time to pry.

I leaned forward, intrigued despite myself. "Tell me more about these Shadowveil Wars. What were they about?"

Reed straightened, his eyes locking onto mine, his expression serious. "The Shadowveil Wars were a series of conflicts that tore Aetheria apart for nearly a century," Reed began. "They started when various factions—mages, witches, shapeshifters, even some rogue fae—began fighting over control of magical ley lines, the very lifeblood of our realm. The war became a breeding ground for dark forces, including a cult that followed Zolothar, a powerful demon from another realm."

Dante cut in, his voice low and serious, a shadow of concern clouding his features. "Zolothar isn't just an ordinary demon. They all hail from a realm far darker than most—a place known as the Umbral Abyss. But Zolothar has always been ambitious. Not content with his place in the Umbral Abyss hierarchy, he sought to rule over realms where he could be uncontested."

"Wow, so this Umbral Abyss is basically hell?" I asked, trying to grasp the enormity of what he was describing.

Dante nodded, his expression somber. "It aligns with Earth lore, yes. It's a home for demons, but it also functions as a prison. It keeps the demons contained and serves as a place to confine other beings who pose a threat to the realms. It's a realm of chaos and despair, filled with demons and malevolent beings constantly vying for power. It's also a place from which escape is nearly impossible. Prisoners can't flee, and demons require either a summoning or a specific type of portal—one that few can open."

Reed nodded, adding, "During the Shadowveil Wars, Zolothar's cult believed they could summon him into Aetheria, intending to use him to dominate both realms. But their attempt failed, causing catastrophic events, including the great fire of the late 1800s here in Savannah."

"Wait..." I blinked, taken aback. "Are you saying that the Savannah fire was caused by a supernatural battle?" My disbelief was evident. "How can that be possible? That's a major event in history!"

Reed chuckled softly, though there was no humor in his eyes. "We work very hard to keep the truth hidden from humans, Little Spark. If you only knew how much of your history has been shaped by our world..."

Giles interjected, sensing my skepticism. "That's exactly why some of us are sentinels, Lenox," he said, his tone grave but patient. "Our job is to keep the balance, to ensure our worlds don't collide in catastrophic ways. Most humans aren't ready to understand the realities of the supernatural—so we keep it from them."

I frowned, trying to process this. "Sentinels? You mean like guardians or protectors?"

Giles nodded. "Precisely. Sentinels are tasked with watching over the fragile borders between our realms. We monitor magical activity, prevent breaches, and—when necessary—intervene to protect both worlds from those who would exploit the gates for their own gain."

I absorbed this new information, my mind reeling. "And you've been doing this...for how long?"

Giles gave a small, almost sad smile. "Long enough to see the damage these breaches can cause. Long enough to know that another conflict like the Shadowveil War would be catastrophic."

I could see the gravity of his words in his eyes, and suddenly, I wanted to know more. "Have you ever...I mean, have you ever faced something like this before?"

"Indeed." Giles's gaze grew distant, his voice quieter. "Once, a long time ago." He hesitated, then continued. "I was still young, not much older than you. There was a breach—a small one, or so we thought. A witch had opened a gate to summon a minor demon for power. We believed we could handle it. But the gate was unstable, tethered to the wrong ley line. It started to tear open, wider and wider, until..." He took a deep breath, the memory clearly painful. "We barely managed to seal it in time. Lost some good friends that day."

The room fell silent. I could feel the weight of his past, the gravity of what it meant to be a sentinel.

Giles shook his head slowly. "That's the thing about these ancient magics. They're unpredictable, volatile. Once unleashed, they're nearly impossible to control, and they always come with a cost."

Reed nodded in agreement, picking up on Giles's point. "After his failed rebellion in the Umbral Abyss, Zolothar was deemed too dangerous even for his own realm. The ancient wardens of Aetheria knew that merely being in the Abyss wasn't enough to contain him. So, they created a pocket realm—a prison within the Abyss itself. This pocket dimension, forged deep within a natural cavern, is bound by powerful Aetherian magic to prevent his escape."

He paused, his fingers drumming against the armrest of his chair. "But even in his imprisonment, his influence can seep through, manipulating those sensitive to his dark energies. The knowledge and methods they used could still be out there, waiting to be rediscovered."

"But why would anyone want that?" I asked, frustration and fear mingling in my voice. "If this demon is so dangerous, why would anyone try to bring him back?"

"Power," Giles interjected, his tone grave. "There are always those who believe they can control forces they don't fully understand, that they'll be the ones to harness it for their gain. It's the same reason cults form in every age—power, ambition, control."

Reed nodded. "There's been an uneasy truce since the end of the Shadowveil War, but it's never truly ended. There have been skirmishes, attempts by different factions to gain power or reignite the conflict. The Cult of Zolothar gains new followers every few decades, no matter how hard the council tries to stamp it out. The war sparks to life every so often because some believe the prophecy that Zolothar will rise again and bring about a new order."

A knot formed in my stomach. "And now...you think the necromancer is trying to reignite that war here?"

Reed's expression was grim. "It's possible. We know the necromancer is raising the dead, and we suspect they're using old, forbidden magic. If they're trying to break the seals, it could be to open a portal—just like before."

Dante leaned forward, his expression grim. "I spoke with my father recently, and he mentioned there's trouble brewing on the eastern border of Aetheria. Some of the old factions are restless again, especially the Drakari. If the gates open now, we could be looking at an all-out war."

Reed's expression grew darker. "The Drakari are on the warpath again? That's the last thing we need. We cannot allow the gates to be opened. Aetheria will erupt, and it will spill over here, causing untold destruction."

Giles nodded, the urgency clear in his voice. "We're down to two suspects who could have both the power and the motive to do this. But we can't afford to wait any longer. We need to act fast."

Reed turned to me, his gaze softening slightly. "Lenox, your ability to communicate with spirits has given us a vital clue and we are all eternally grateful. Now, it's up to us to act on it."

I nodded, my resolve hardening. "Then let's do it. What's the plan?"

Reed gave a firm nod and turned to Giles. "Giles, you, Lenox, and your detective friend continue chasing down the suspects. Dante and I will make preparations on our end in case the worst happens. The fires of the past must not be allowed to rise again."

22

DREAMS AND DOUBTS

*T*he room was dark, save for the slivers of moonlight streaming through the tall, narrow windows. My footsteps echoed softly on the cold marble floor, the sound somehow louder in the oppressive silence. I knew this place, yet I didn't. It felt like a memory trapped in the haze of a forgotten dream.

A gallery. Paintings lined the walls—works of art both beautiful and haunting. I was drawn to them, compelled to examine each one. As I moved closer to a large painting of a moonlit forest, the details began to change, shifting and twisting under my gaze.

The trees seemed to sway, their branches reaching out like skeletal hands, and the darkness between them deepened, becoming an abyss.

My heart pounded in my chest, a feeling of dread washing over me. I turned, intending to move away, but my feet wouldn't budge.

Panic gripped me, cold and relentless. The painting wasn't just a painting anymore. It was alive.

Suddenly, the room shifted around me, the walls melting away like wet paint on a canvas. I was no longer in the gallery. I was outside, in a dense forest, the full moon casting a pale, ghostly light on the path ahead.

The air was thick with mist, and the scent of pine filled my lungs. I looked down and saw I was wearing a gown—a beautiful, intricate ball gown, the fabric shimmering with an otherworldly glow.

An Ouroboros—the snake eating its own tail—wound around the skirt, with the head and tail meeting just below my waist. Its emerald eyes glinted in the moonlight, urging me to touch it.

With a will of its own, my hand moved closer and trembling fingers stroked the serpent's head. In a flash of light, the Ouroboros came to life, wrapping around my wrist with an iron grip. Bile rose in my throat as the scales undulated against my skin.

Run!

The word echoed in my mind, a command I didn't fully understand but couldn't resist. I took off, the gown's cumbersome fabric tangling around my legs as I stumbled through the underbrush.

The forest was alive with shadows, shapes moving just beyond my line of sight.

A rustle behind me, a branch snapping—I didn't dare look back. My breath came in ragged gasps, fear driving me forward. But I could feel him gaining on me, his presence like a dark cloud closing in. Julian.

I didn't know how I knew it was him, but I did. He was there, chasing me, his eyes filled with something I couldn't quite place—determination, maybe desperation.

"Julian, please!" I screamed, my voice breaking. But he didn't stop. He kept coming, his footsteps relentless, unyielding.

Julian was gaining, his footsteps pounding closer and closer. I could feel the earth tremble beneath each step, or maybe it was my own fear shaking me to my core.

My breath came in short, ragged gasps, each one burning my throat like fire. My lungs screamed for air, my legs ached with every desperate stride, but I couldn't stop.

I had to keep going, had to escape. Panic clawed at my insides, twisting my stomach into knots. Why was he chasing me? What did he want? The questions echoed in my mind, but I had no answers, only the primal urge to survive.

Branches tore at my gown and scratched my skin, but I barely felt the pain through the adrenaline. My heart hammered in my chest, a frantic drumbeat that drowned out everything else.

A sob caught in my throat as I stumbled, nearly falling, the ground slick with leaves and mud. Julian's voice called out, low and urgent, but I couldn't make out the words.

Was he warning me? Threatening me? I couldn't tell, and I didn't dare look back. The fear was all-consuming, a cold knot in my gut kept me running, fleeing from whatever fate awaited me if I was caught.

The Ouroboros around my wrist began to glow, its scales tightening further, almost painful now. I could feel its energy coursing through me, a strange, foreign power that both terrified and thrilled me.

Suddenly, Julian lunged, his hand outstretched, his fingers brushing against the fabric of my gown. I tried to scream again, but the sound died in my throat as I stumbled and fell, the world spinning around me.

As I hit the ground, the forest seemed to close in, the trees leaning forward as if to swallow me whole. Julian's face loomed above me, his features contorted with something dark and unreadable. The

Ouroboros clamped down harder, its glow intensifying, blinding. My wrist burned like it was branding me, searing through my skin, and then—

I woke with a start, gasping for breath, my heart pounding wildly in my chest. The dim light of early morning filtered through the curtains, casting long shadows on the walls of my bedroom.

My sheets were tangled around me, damp with sweat. I glanced at my wrist, half-expecting to see the Ouroboros still there, but of course, it wasn't. Just the faint outline of a red mark where it had been in the dream.

What the hell was that? I thought, as I pressed a hand to my chest, trying to steady the frantic beat of my heart. I ran a shaky hand through my hair, my mind racing.

The dream was different this time, more vivid, more intense. And Julian—why was he there? Why was he chasing me?

I shook my head, trying to shake off the lingering dread. Julian had never done anything to make me doubt him, had he? He was kind, caring, always attentive. So why had my subconscious twisted him into something dark and menacing?

Maybe it was the stress, I reasoned, pushing the thoughts aside. My mind was playing tricks on me, blending the fear I felt about the necromancer with someone who had only been supportive.

A sharp beep broke through my thoughts, making me jump. I reached for my phone on the bedside table, my fingers fumbling as I swiped the screen.

A text from Julian. *Good morning, beautiful! Breakfast at La Paloma? Good food and my scintillating company. No better way to start the day!*

I stared at the screen, my mind still reeling from the dream. Part of me wanted to ignore the message, to avoid him altogether after what I'd just experienced.

But it was just a dream, wasn't it? Nothing more than a manifestation of my overactive imagination and the stress of everything happening around me. Besides, Julian had been nothing but kind.

I started to type an acceptance when Giles's warning about not going anywhere alone echoed in my mind. *Not alone,*

Lenox, not even for a minute. My thumb hovered over the screen. Giles had bent his rule in regard to my guiding tours and this was also in a public place, I reasoned. Plus, it was daylight, and Marco's bistro was always bustling with people.

With a small sigh, I typed back:

Sounds good, but I have to make it a quick one. Meeting with Giles right after. 7:30 work? I hit send before I could second-guess myself.

Almost immediately, a reply came through. *7:30 it is! Looking forward to it. You're saving me from a very pitiful morning of eating alone.*

I couldn't help but smile. Poor Julian, I thought, but I couldn't deny I was looking forward to seeing him again, even if just for a short while. I just needed to keep my guard up—Giles was right. The necromancer wasn't playing games.

The aroma of freshly brewed coffee and warm pastries greeted me as I stepped into La Paloma. The small café was already buzzing with early morning patrons—locals grabbing their caffeine fix before heading off to work, a couple of tourists poring over maps and brochures.

I spotted Julian sitting at a small table near the window, his back to the wall, a view of the entire room before him. He looked up as I approached, a bright smile breaking across his face. "Lenox! Right on time."

I smiled back, sliding into the chair opposite him. "I aim to please."

He laughed, his eyes sparkling with good humor. "I took the liberty of ordering you a cappuccino and a croissant. Hope that's okay."

"Perfect, thank you," I replied, feeling a bit more at ease. Julian had a way of making everything seem light and carefree, a stark contrast to the dark, oppressive thoughts that had been plaguing me.

As we settled into the familiar rhythm of casual conversation, Julian leaned back in his chair, a thoughtful expression on his face. "I've been working on a new exhibit," he began, his tone casual but with a hint of excitement.

"It's called *Ethereal Echoes*. It focuses on works that capture the ephemeral nature of existence—light, shadow, memory. I think you'd really appreciate it."

I nodded, intrigued despite myself. "Sounds fascinating. When is it opening?"

"A couple of weeks," Julian replied, his eyes lighting up. "I'd love for you to come to the private showing. It's going to be a small gathering, just a few patrons and artists, a chance to see the pieces up close before the public does."

"I'll think about it," I said, trying to keep my tone light. The idea of being in an art gallery again, surrounded by paintings, felt both inviting and unnerving. I wasn't sure I was ready for that.

Julian nodded, a small smile playing at his lips. "I understand. No pressure. It's just, I'm excited to share this with you...bringing this exhibit to Savannah was a bit of a splurge. Costly, but worth it, I think."

I tilted my head, curiosity piqued. "Costly? I thought exhibits were usually quite profitable for galleries?"

Julian chuckled softly, but there was a fleeting shadow in his eyes. "They can be, but there's a lot of upfront investment—shipping, insurance, securing the right pieces. Sometimes it feels like I'm pouring everything back into the business just to keep it running smoothly."

I offered a sympathetic nod, though a small part of me couldn't help but wonder. Julian always seemed so confident, so assured in his success. To hear him speak of the gallery this way was... different.

"Well, I'm sure it'll be a success," I said, trying to lift the mood. "And I'll definitely try to make it to the showing."

Julian's smile returned, brighter this time. "I'd love that, Lenox. It would mean a lot to me." He reached into his bag and pulled out a sleek brochure, sliding it across the table to me. "On another note, Victor is assisting me with the exhibit, and he asked about you. He's really impressed with your talent and wanted me to give you this."

I glanced down at the brochure, my name printed neatly on the front cover. It was an invitation to the summer art classes. A flutter of something—excitement? Anxiety?—stirred inside me. I wasn't sure.

"What do you think?" Julian asked, his gaze earnest. "Will you take the classes? I think it could be a great opportunity for you to explore your abilities."

I brushed off his question with a noncommittal shrug. "I'll think about it," I repeated, folding the brochure and tucking it into my bag. I didn't want to admit to him, or to myself, that the idea of picking up a paintbrush again scared me.

The truth was, something stirred in me at the idea, something deep and unfamiliar. But it felt too foreign, too distant from the chaos my life was currently wrapped in. Now wasn't the time to be taking on anything new.

Sensing my reluctance, Julian smoothly shifted the conversation. "Did you hear about the new mural project downtown? They're looking for volunteers to help with the design. It's supposed to be a community effort, capturing the spirit of Savannah."

I nodded, grateful for the change in subject. "I heard about it. Sounds like a great project."

Julian's voice faded into the background as my mind drifted, the nightmare from earlier still lingering at the edges of my thoughts. I kept seeing his face from the dream—his expression, so different from the man sitting across from me now. It was hard to reconcile the two images, to remind myself that dreams weren't reality.

"Lenox?" Julian's voice pulled me back, his expression concerned. "You okay?"

I blinked, focusing on him again. "Sorry, just...lost in thought."

He smiled softly. "Anything you want to share?"

I hesitated, then shook my head. "No, just thinking about work."

Julian nodded, accepting my answer, though his eyes remained on me, searching. "Well, I hope you can make some time for fun, too. Life's too short to be all work and no play."

I forced a smile, though my mind was still racing. "I'll try," I promised, though I wasn't sure I believed it myself.

We finished our breakfast, the conversation flowing easily despite my distraction. Julian was charming, as always, and by the time I glanced at my watch, I realized I was cutting it close.

"I should go," I said, standing up. "I've got to meet Giles and Derek."

Julian stood as well, his expression disappointed but understanding. "Of course. But let's do this again soon, okay?"

I nodded, smiling. "Sure. I'll let you know when I have some free time."

He walked me to the door, his hand lightly resting on the small of my back. "Take care, Lenox," he said softly, his eyes lingering on mine for a moment longer than necessary.

"You too, Julian," I replied, stepping out into the morning sun, the cool breeze a welcome contrast to the warmth of the café.

As I walked away, I couldn't help but glance back, seeing him still watching me from the doorway, a strange expression on his face—part longing, part something else I couldn't quite place.

With a deep breath, I turned my focus back to the day ahead. Whatever Julian's intentions, I had bigger things to worry about. The necromancer was still out there, and time was running out.

I left with dread and resolve swirling in my chest. Julian had been a welcome distraction, but I couldn't let myself get too comfortable. As I crossed Monterey Square, the weight of everything we'd discussed the previous night pressed down on me. I hurried toward Giles's house, its imposing facade looming ahead.

Inside, the house was quiet, save for the low hum of voices from the study. I pushed the door open, stepping inside to find Giles and Derek already deep in conversation.

Giles looked up as I entered, his gaze immediately scrutinizing. "I trust you weren't out and about alone?" he asked, half-joking, half-serious.

I shook my head, a small smile on my lips. "Don't worry, Giles. I wasn't alone. I had breakfast at Marco's."

He raised an eyebrow, a hint of a smile playing on his lips. "With Julian, I presume?"

"Yes, and don't worry. I kept it short," I assured him. "I remembered what you said. Public places, lots of people."

Giles nodded approvingly. "Good. Just...be careful, Lenox. We're dealing with forces far beyond our usual."

Derek chimed in, glancing between us. "So, what's the plan? We know Samuel's nearby. Are we heading there first?"

Giles nodded, looking serious. "Yes. Given his proximity and history, he's our best bet to start with. If he's involved, we can't afford to waste time."

Derek pulled out his phone, checking his messages. "Let's get moving, then. With everything you told me about this Shadowveil War and demons, I'd say time is not on our side."

Just as we were about to leave, Derek's phone buzzed again, his expression shifting from urgency to frustration. "Damn it. Officer-involved shooting. I have to go."

Giles waved him off. "Go. We'll handle this."

Derek nodded, already moving. "Be safe," he called over his shoulder.

I turned to Giles, a determined look in my eyes. "Just us, then?"

"Just us," Giles confirmed. "Let's get going. I've got the car in the garage."

We headed out to the garage, where a sleek Aston Martin waited. I stared at it, momentarily caught off guard by the surprise.

"You've been hiding this?" I asked, half-laughing, half-impressed.

Giles chuckled. "It's good to have a few surprises up my sleeve."

"Clearly," I said, sliding into the passenger seat. "Let's see what this baby can do."

He started the engine, and as the car roared to life, a renewed sense of determination surged within me. Today, we would find some answers. Today, we would take the next step toward uncovering the truth.

23

DEAD
RECKONING

S amuel's boat storage facility sat on a deep-water
canal at the edge of Talahi Island. The sun was still
rising, casting sharp shadows across the isolated property. Despite the daylight, an unsettling stillness lingered,
the dense thickets and abandoned structures creating the
perfect cover for something—or someone.

The property was enclosed by a fence, the house on it ne-
glected and faded. Behind it, a large pole barn stood along
the water, its peeling paint and dark windows making my
skin crawl.

"Looks vacant," Giles muttered, cutting the engine and
grabbing his messenger bag. "There's a car here, though.
Let's check it out."

We knocked on the front door. No answer. Another knock, harder this time—nothing but silence. Then, a sudden clang from behind the house—the sound of a heavy metal door slamming.

Giles and I exchanged a look. "That came from the back," I whispered.

We moved cautiously around the house, stepping into a gravel lot. The barn loomed ahead, flickering light seeping through its cracks. The air was thick with the acrid taste of magic. It clung to my tongue, sour like copper.

"Someone's definitely using magic," I muttered.

Giles nodded, hand slipping into his bag, his expression grim. I let out a nervous laugh. "Prepared as always?"

He managed a tight smile. "Can't be too careful."

As we neared the barn's side door, the stench hit us—overpowering and rancid. I gagged, covering my mouth. "What the hell is that?"

Giles grimaced. "Only one way to find out." He pulled the door open, and the smell hit harder, making my eyes water. I stepped inside, blinking against the dim, flickering light—and gasped.

There they were—row upon row of figures standing in perfect formation. Zombies. Their eyes were vacant, skin hanging loose and rotting, but they were all standing upright, unmoving, as if waiting for a command.

"Dear God..." I whispered, the horror of the scene sinking in.

"They're in stasis," Giles said quietly, his voice low and tense. "Waiting for instructions." He took a deep breath, his eyes scanning the warehouse. "We've definitely found our necromancer."

As I got closer, I saw the remnants of who they once were—tattered clothes that might have been a favorite dress, a tarnished wedding band still clinging to a withered finger.

My steps faltered. These had been people with lives, families... dreams. I pressed a hand to my mouth, fighting the urge to vomit.

"What kind of person could do this?" I murmured. "Can they be...put to rest?"

Before Giles could answer, a voice rang out from the shadows. "Oh, they have a much greater purpose than being worm food." Samuel stepped into view, a twisted grin on his face. "My creations will deliver my enemies up for slaughter, and I will have my revenge!"

Samuel's greasy black hair clung to his forehead, his sharp, ferret-like features twisted in a sneer. His wild eyes gleamed with a sick, unhinged light. The sight of him filled me with dread, tightening in my chest like a vice.

"Samuel," Giles commanded, his voice low and firm. "You've desecrated the dead and twisted the natural order. It's over. Stop this now or face the consequences. There's no place left for you to hide—not in this world, or any other."

Samuel's grin widened. "Oh, you think it's over? No, my friends. It's only just beginning." He raised his arms, chanting in a guttural language that sent a shiver down my spine. The zombies around us began to stir, their eyes lighting up with an eerie green glow.

"Giles! He's activating them!" I shouted, my voice trembling as the zombies began to lurch forward, their movements slow but deliberate.

"Head for the exit!" Giles commanded, urgency sharpening his tone.

I whipped around, heart racing, and sprinted toward the door, but skidded to a stop as I saw it—blocked by a wall of zombies, their blank eyes fixed on us. "It's blocked!" I called back.

Giles muttered a curse, scanning the room. "Stay close!" he ordered, reaching into his bag. In one swift motion, he pulled out a bundle of sage and flicked a lighter. The sage ignited, releasing a thin plume of smoke.

"Back up!" he instructed. I followed his gaze and saw that we were being herded into a corner of the warehouse, where a few dusty chairs were stacked haphazardly against the wall.

He waved the smoldering sage in front of us, creating a barrier of fragrant smoke. For a moment, the zombies hesitated, their steps faltering. The scent filled the air, sharp and herbal, and I could sense a slight shift in the atmosphere, a momentary pause in the advancing horde.

"Buy us some time!" Giles yelled, tossing the smoldering sage at the nearest zombies. Thick smoke curled up, creating a barrier that made them hesitate, their blank expressions faltering.

I grabbed a chair and swung it at the closest zombie, the legs cracking against its skull. It staggered back, but more pressed forward, pushing through the haze.

Giles dropped to his knees, pulling out a piece of chalk. With quick, precise movements, he began drawing a circle around us. "Keep them back, Lenox! Almost there!"

I swung the chair again, adrenaline surging as another zombie lurched toward me. It stumbled but kept coming. "Come on, Giles!" I shouted, panic edging my voice. "Hurry!"

Giles's hand moved faster, his face slick with sweat. "Nearly done!" he muttered as the circle glowed faintly, the last sigil taking form.

The zombies were closing in, their rotting hands reaching out. I swung the chair with everything I had. "Giles! I can't hold them off much longer!"

Desperate, I glanced at Samuel, standing in the repair bay with his arms spread wide, chanting, his eyes gleaming with madness. An idea struck—if I could distract him, maybe it would slow the zombies.

"Samuel!" I yelled, knocking down another zombie. "Why are you doing this? What do you stand to gain from all this chaos?"

His chanting faltered, his eyes flicking toward me. "What's it to you, girl?" he sneered.

I had his attention, at least for a moment. "Is this really about revenge?" I pressed. I needed to keep him talking, keep him focused on me instead of Giles. "Desecrating the dead, attacking people—because you're a pathetic little man who couldn't handle a time out?"

Samuel's face twisted with fury. "Pathetic? This is about power! The council cast me out because I dared to wield magic they feared!" His anger slowed the zombies, their movements becoming sluggish.

I glanced at Giles, who was finishing the protective circle. He straightened, dusting off his hands. "That should hold the undead."

But Samuel's eyes gleamed with sudden realization. "Nice try," he sneered. "You think you can distract me that easily?"

Samuel's voice rose in a dark chant, weaving intricate patterns in the air. Shadows in the warehouse pulsed and grew, a wave of icy dread washing over me.

Giles's face paled. "Oh no..."

From the shadows, guttural growls echoed. Dark shapes emerged, eyes glowing sickly yellow. They moved with predatory grace, circling us.

"What does 'oh no' mean?" I asked, panic rising.

"Ghouls," Giles replied grimly. "Stronger, faster than zombies. And they're hungry."

A wave of dread washed over me. "What do we do?"

Giles quickly dug into his bag, pulling out a small, ornate vial of blessed water. The liquid shimmered faintly. "Lenox, this should keep them back, but only for a moment." He uncorked the vial and flung the glowing water in a wide arc around us.

The water hit the ground with a sizzle, an acrid smell filling the air. The ghouls recoiled, hissing and snarling as the water formed a faint barrier of light. I watched in awe as it held them back, if only temporarily.

The ghouls snapped their jaws, pacing along the barrier's edge. I could see the light flickering, struggling to maintain its form.

"We don't have much time," Giles muttered, rummaging through his bag. "Lenox, keep them distracted! I need to find something stronger!"

I gripped the chair tighter. "Distract them, right," I muttered, eyeing the advancing ghouls and zombies. "Add 'ghoul wrangler' to my resume."

I swung the chair again, muscles aching with each strike. The ghouls were undeterred, their eyes locked on us with a hunger that turned my blood to ice.

Giles's hands fumbled in his bag, his face drawn with concentration. "If I can just find... Ah! There it is." He pulled out a small vial filled with a thick, dark liquid. "I need a few minutes to work this spell, Lenox."

I swung the chair in a desperate arc, knocking back a zombie that had gotten too close. But the ghouls were closing in, their growls deepening, their eyes glowing brighter with each step.

Panic surged. "Giles, whatever you're planning, do it fast!"

Just as I was ready to give in to despair, a familiar cold washed over me. I turned and saw Amelia, her ethereal form glowing with a soft blue light.

"Lenox!" she called, her voice echoing in my mind. "Join with me! We can fight them together!"

I reached out, grabbing her hand. A surge of powerful, intoxicating energy flowed between us. Amelia's presence solidified, and with a flash of light, she sent a wave of energy crashing into the advancing zombies and ghouls, knocking them back.

I exhaled, a shaky breath I hadn't realized I was holding. My legs felt like jelly, and for the first time, hope flickered in my chest. "Amelia, that was amazing! Like bowling for zombies!"

Before we could celebrate, Samuel's voice cut through the air. "You think that's all I've got?" he sneered, raising his arms. The ground trembled as he began weaving another spell, a smug smile curling his lips.

Amelia's grip tightened on my hand, her energy surging through me. "Lenox, you need to open a portal. Now."

"Wh-what?" I stammered, panic and confusion rising. "I don't know how to do that!"

"Yes, you do," Amelia insisted. "It's why he's been trying to control you! You have the power to open the gates! Concentrate."

I froze, fear constricting my chest. *A portal? How was I supposed to know how to do that?*

But as the words sank in, memories flooded back—the shimmering distortion I'd seen on River Street when the zombie attacked, and again at the bookstore window right before the strange surge of energy.

I had dismissed them as tricks of the light, hallucinations even. But they hadn't been. They were real. And they were connected to me.

"Lenox," Amelia urged, "you've done it before, even if you didn't know it. Focus on those moments. You can do this."

I squeezed my eyes shut, summoning the memory of those instances—the ripple in the air, the way reality itself had seemed to twist. I hadn't known what it was then, but now, I had to make it happen on purpose. I focused harder, trying to recreate the shimmer in my mind but I wasn't sure if I had anything left to give.

My body was drained, my mind spinning. But with the ghouls circling, I couldn't stop. I had to try, for Giles, for Amelia, for all of us.

Giles's voice cut through. "It's working, Lenox! Make it stronger!"

My heart pounded in my ears, and my thoughts scrambled. How could I focus through this exhaustion? The energy swirling inside me felt wild and untamed, ready to rip me apart if I lost control for even a second.

"How?" I huffed, exhaustion washing over me.

"Focus on the image! Channel your fear, your anger—everything—into light. Now push it into the portal!"

I swallowed hard and focused on all my fear, my frustration, and my anger, letting it build into a glowing ball of light in my mind. It pulsed, growing hotter, brighter, more intense.

The ground beneath us began to tremble. "That's it, Lenox!" Giles gasped. "Keep going! You're doing it!"

Breathless and weak, I gathered everything I had left, forcing the glowing light toward the shimmer, willing it to break through. The air around us crackled with raw power.

I opened my eyes to see it—a swirling vortex spiraled downward, glowing with an eerie energy. Through it, I could see a barren, desolate landscape pulsing with malevolent force.

"The Umbral Abyss," I whispered, a mixture of awe and dread in my voice. I had done it. I had opened a portal to another realm.

The zombies, caught in the swirling energy, were drawn toward it, stumbling and tripping over one another. I could hear Giles muttering, completing the final sigils on whatever spell he'd found to use against the ghouls.

"The Umbral Abyss," Amelia whispered. "We can send him to hell..."

Samuel's eyes widened, and a twisted grin spread across his face. "You've opened the gate... Perfect!" he crowed. Without missing a beat, he began a new incantation, his voice rising in a dark, commanding tone.

His hands moved in intricate patterns, and I could feel a shift in the air—a pull toward the portal. "Now, my army marches to Aetheria!"

But as the portal continued to swirl, his expression shifted, confusion flickering across his features. He squinted at the vortex, realization dawning. "Wait...this isn't...where does this lead?" His voice turned sharp, accusatory. "What realm have you opened?"

Amelia's grip on my hand tightened. As the power surged from me into Amelia, I felt it like a wave crashing against rocks. My legs buckled under the force, every inch of my body screaming in protest. I tried to hold on, but the strength was slipping away faster than I could catch my breath.

"Amelia, what are you—"

She didn't answer. Dropping my hand, she crept up behind Samuel, her face set with fierce determination. He was too engrossed in his incantation to notice. Just as he began to speak, Amelia shoved him from behind.

Samuel stumbled; his eyes wide with shock as he lost his balance. He toppled into the portal, a scream tearing from his lips as he fell into the abyss.

For a moment, there was silence. Amelia stood with her back to it, a triumphant smile. "It's over," she whispered. "He's gone."

But before she could step away, a hand shot out from the swirling mass—a bony, clawed hand that grabbed her ankle.

"Amelia!" I screamed, rushing forward. I grabbed her hand, trying to pull her back, but I was weak, my strength nearly gone. The portal's edges began to fray, struggling to remain open.

Samuel's voice echoed from within the abyss, twisted with malice. "You think you can defeat me so easily?" His hand pulled at Amelia, dragging her toward the depths.

"Lenox!" Amelia gasped. "He's trying to pull himself back out. You have to let me go. You have to close the portal!"

"I won't let you fall into that place!" I cried. "There must be another way! Just—just vanish like you did before. Turn into vapor or something!"

Amelia shook her head, her eyes wide with desperation. "I can't! There's too much of your life force still in me. I'm bound to this plane—I can't leave until it dissipates."

My heart pounded. I couldn't let her fall into that hellish abyss. Then I felt it—a sudden tug—Amelia's body sliding farther toward the portal. I tightened my grip but Samuel's full weight was dragging her down, pulling her closer to the edge as she strained to hold on.

"Lenox," Amelia's eyes met mine with a sad resolve. "Let me go. I'm already dead. This is justice."

Tears streamed down my face as I shook my head, trying to pull her back. "No, please...don't make me do this."

Amelia's gaze softened. "Thank you, Lenox. For everything. But this...this is my choice."

I could feel the last of my energy slipping away, the portal beginning to falter. "No!" I sobbed, but my grip was weakening. I knew she was right, but the thought of letting go...

"Lenox," Amelia whispered, firm. "Let me go. This is the end I choose."

My grip on her hand loosened, my mind screaming at me to hold on tighter, to never let go. But deep down, I knew she was right. There was no other way, and yet...

"Please, Amelia," I choked out. "Not like this." But her eyes held mine, filled with quiet, resolute strength.

For a moment, it felt like our hearts beat in sync. I didn't want to let her go, but I knew—I had to trust her.

With a final, tearful nod, I released her hand, my heart breaking as I watched her fall back toward the portal. Her *thank you* carried on the wind as she disappeared into the swirling darkness of the Umbral Abyss.

And then, just as suddenly as it had appeared, the portal closed with a deafening snap, the warehouse falling silent. The silence pressed in, heavy and absolute, as if the world itself had paused to acknowledge what had just happened.

I fell to my knees, tears streaming down my face, the weight of Amelia's sacrifice settling over me like a shroud.

24
FALLOUT

Three days had passed since the battle, yet the memory of it lingered in my mind like a persistent shadow. Giles' study was cozy, the fire crackling softly in the hearth, warding off the gloom of a rainy and overcast day.

I perched on the edge of one of the wingback chairs, my thoughts swirling as I prepared to recount what had happened. The others waited expectantly, their faces showing both concern and curiosity.

I took a deep breath, choosing my words carefully. "We found him," I began, my voice steady despite the turmoil inside. "Samuel, he'd been using his storage building to hide his army of zombies."

Giles nodded. "It makes sense. He wouldn't have wanted to draw too much attention to himself, and the stench would have alerted neighbors had he had any."

Everyone murmured agreement, then Reed leaned forward, his eyes narrowing. "Did he give any indication of his motive?"

I glanced at Giles, then back at the others. "It was revenge," I explained. "He was angry with the council of Aetheria. He blamed them for everything—his exile, the loss of his work...his whole life."

Dante sighed, shaking his head. "That sounds like Samuel. Even in Aetheria, he pushed boundaries, broke rules. When the council shut him down, it must have felt like a death sentence."

Reed's face tightened. "He wanted to prove he wasn't a failure, that he still had power. That kind of obsession can drive a person to madness."

I nodded. "He wanted to show everyone he was still powerful, that he wasn't to be underestimated. But in the end, his need for power destroyed him."

Giles added, "He thought he could control dark forces, but instead, they consumed him. He underestimated the very magic he sought to wield."

Reed's gaze shifted to me, his expression thoughtful. "And Amelia...is her soul at peace now?"

A lump formed in my throat; the memory of Amelia's sacrifice still raw. "She...she gave herself to close the portal, to stop Samuel from bringing something worse through. She...saved us all."

The room fell into a respectful silence, her sacrifice weighing on everyone. Finally, I broke the stillness, my voice firm. "We can't just leave her there. We have to find a way to bring her back."

Dante's expression softened, but his tone remained serious. "Lenox, remember I told you the Umbral Abyss is a prison? It's a one-way door. No one has ever returned from there."

I clenched my fists, refusing to back down. "I refuse to accept that. If I could open the gate from this side, then maybe I can figure out a way to open it from the other."

Derek, who had been quietly observing, leaned forward. "Lenox, how *did* you open that portal? That's beyond talking to ghosts."

The room fell silent again, all eyes on me. I fidgeted under their scrutiny. "It was Amelia," I said softly. "She told me I could do it. I didn't believe her at first, but she insisted. I realized I'd accidentally done it before and well"—I shrugged— "I did it again."

"What?" Reed's eyebrows shot up. "Accidentally? You're telling me you've opened gates before? When? Where did this happen?"

His sharp tone made me flinch. Reed was usually so composed, but now, he seemed almost...angry. My heart pounded in my chest, anxiety tightening its grip. I knew he wasn't angry at me, not really, but his intensity was unnerving. What if I'd done something terribly wrong? What if this power was more dangerous than I realized?

I hesitated, my gaze flicking to Giles for reassurance, but his expression was unreadable. Swallowing hard, I took a deep breath, trying to steady my voice. "The first time was as I passed the bookstore," I said slowly, watching Reed's face for any sign of softening. "The second time was on River Street when the zombies attacked."

Reed's eyes narrowed, his posture rigid. "And you did this"— he snapped his fingers—"just like that?"

His dismissive gesture and accusatory tone sent a jolt of irritation through me. My face flushed under his harsh glare. Who was he to judge?

Since the day we met, Reed had a way of getting under my skin, pushing my buttons just enough to set me on edge. And now he looked at me like I was some reckless child who'd played with fire.

I lifted my chin, my voice sharpening in response to his. "Yes, accidentally," I shot back. "As in, not on purpose. It just... happened."

I crossed my arms over my chest, glaring at him. "There was a zombie horde intent on killing us all, Reed. I wasn't exactly in the mood to think things through because I was a little busy not dying!"

A tense silence settled over the room, their gazes flicking between us like they were watching a tennis match. Reed opened his mouth to retort, his expression hardening, but Dante swiftly cut in.

"Hey, hey, both of you, back to your corners." Dante raised his hands as if refereeing a boxing match. His tone was light, but there was a hint of steel beneath it. "Let's take a breath here, alright?"

Reed shot Dante a look, his jaw tight, but he took a step back, exhaling sharply. The tension in my shoulders eased, my pulse still racing but beginning to settle.

Dante's steady presence was like a balm, soothing the frayed edges of my nerves.

"Lenox," Dante continued, turning his attention to me, his expression softer, more understanding. "Reed's just worried, that's all. And you"—he glanced at Reed—"could maybe try not to sound like an interrogator from the Inquisition?"

Reed's lips twitched, a reluctant smile breaking through his stern facade. "Alright, alright," he conceded, a touch of warmth returning to his eyes as he looked at me.

"I'm sorry, Lenox. I didn't mean to come down on you so hard. It's just...this power you have, it's not something to take lightly. It's dangerous, especially if it's triggered by strong emotions, which is what it sounds like."

I uncrossed my arms, relief mingled with lingering frustration. "I get it, Reed. But it's not like I asked for this." I huffed. "I don't even know how I did it!"

Reed nodded; his tone gentler now, like he was trying to calm a skittish colt. "I know, and that's why you need training. If you can learn to control it, you can turn this into an asset instead of a liability."

Giles nodded, a thoughtful look on his face. "Lenox, you have a gift that needs honing. Reed is right about the dangers of an uncontrolled power like yours. We can't afford any more accidental gates opening to God knows where."

He paused, his eyes sharpening with concern. "And worse still, if left unchecked, this could bring things through that shouldn't be here at all."

I frowned, chewing over his words. "Gift?" I repeated, a touch of skepticism in my voice. "How did I even get this. ..gift? I mean, opening portals? That's not exactly normal, is it?"

Reed leaned against the fireplace mantel. "No, it's not. In fact, very few can open gates like the ones you've opened, and those who can are usually highly trained mages or beings with inherent magical ties."

He tilted his head to one side, eyes narrowing slightly, as if trying to solve a riddle that didn't quite make sense. His tone was thoughtful as he mused. "The fact that you've done it unintentionally, twice, suggests..." He frowned and leaned closer. "Who are your parents? Where did you grow up? Maybe there were ley lines nearby or some ancestor was..."

I squirmed under his intense gaze. My heart pounded in my chest and irritation bubbled up. "Why do you always look at me like that?" I blurted out, my frustration getting the better of me. "Like I'm some kind of bug under a microscope?"

Reed blinked, clearly taken aback. He opened his mouth, then closed it, his brow furrowing. "I don't..." he started, but the words faltered.

He huffed and tried again, his voice uncertain. "I mean, it's not like I...that's not..." He stammered, then let out a frustrated sigh, rubbing the back of his neck before turning those piercing blue eyes on me. "Didn't you ever stop to wonder *why* I was looking at you like that?"

I blinked, taken aback by his outburst. As his accusation sank in, I offered a small shrug and admitted, a bit sheepishly, "I just thought you were being...impudent."

His eyebrows shot up, a slow grin spreading across his face. "You think I'm...impudent?"

The room chuckled softly, and my face flamed. I shot him a glare. "Being bold as brass isn't a compliment, you idiot." I rolled my eyes and shook my head. "Don't let it go to your head."

Reed's grin widened, but there was a glint of something more—something almost teasing—in his eyes. "Too late for that, Little Spark."

Giles cleared his throat and chuckled softly, a hint of indulgence in his tone. "Alright, you two," he said with a gentle smile. "Let's bring it back to the point."

"Agreed, Giles." Reed grinned and winked at me. "Your humor aside, Little Spark, we do need to understand more about where these abilities come from."

"It's imperative that we do so!" Giles added. "Lenox, your gifts aren't just a curiosity—they're powerful, and without control, they can be dangerous. We need to understand what we're dealing with here."

"Which is why we're trying to figure you out," Reed said, his gaze softening slightly. "The fact that you've done it three times, intentionally or not, suggests there's more to your heritage than we know."

My heart skipped a beat. "Heritage?" The word hung in the air, and my mind flashed back to Alaric's voice, cold and sharp, calling me an abomination. I could almost feel the weight of that accusation again, like a brand seared into my soul.

And then Maris, her sneer twisting as she spat the word rogue like I was some wild animal that needed taming. They had both implied the same thing—that I wasn't fully human, that there was something inherently wrong with me.

Fear and frustration surged inside me. "So, what are you saying? That I'm some kind of freak of nature?"

Giles shook his head, his expression softening. "No, not a freak, Lenox. But there's definitely something unique about you. Maybe it's in your family line, something we haven't uncovered yet."

Dante chimed in, his voice gentler. "Normal is a relative term, Lenox. In our world, normal covers a wide spectrum. You're discovering more about yourself, that's all. And sometimes, the most extraordinary abilities come from the most unexpected places."

I took a deep breath, letting Dante's words sink in, but a thought gnawed at the edge of my mind. "But how am I supposed to figure out my heritage when I can't even remember my own past?"

Reed's eyes narrowed in surprise. "What do you mean, you can't remember?"

The room's focus shifted again, all eyes landing on me. I hesitated, feeling the pressure of their attention. This wasn't how I wanted to share my past, but they needed to know.

My chest tightened. "I...I don't remember anything about my life before I woke up from a coma and moved to Savannah," I admitted, my voice trembling slightly. "I had an accident, and when I came to, everything from before was...gone."

As I said the words, the familiar wave of anxiety crept up my spine. Would they pity me? Would they look at me like I was broken? I hated being the one who didn't have answers, the one with gaps in my past like a puzzle missing its most important pieces.

The idea that they'd see me as a liability, a problem that needed solving, gnawed at me. But worst of all was the fear that I'd never remember—that I'd never truly know who I was.

Reed's face shifted from curiosity to shock. "You're telling me you have no memories of who you are? Nothing?"

I nodded, sensing the intensity of his gaze. "Nothing. Just flashes, sometimes dreams that don't make sense. I don't even know my real name."

You could have heard a pin drop. Everyone's expressions shifted from confusion to shock, and maybe a hint of pity. I hated the pity in their eyes. I wasn't a charity case. I wasn't looking for sympathy. I needed answers. Answers only my lost memories could provide.

Reed's expression shifted from curiosity to shock. His confident demeanor faltered, and for a moment, he just stared at me, processing what I'd said. His hands, usually so controlled, clenched and unclenched as if searching for a grip on this new reality.

The silence stretched out as if he was struggling to find the right words. A flicker of something crossed his face. I hadn't expected that look—like I'd just pulled the rug out from under him. He blinked, as if trying to reconcile his earlier suspicion with this new, unsettling truth.

His shoulders seemed to sag slightly, the tension draining from his posture, and his blue eyes, usually so sharp and sure, now searched my face for a truth I didn't have.

In that brief pause, I saw him differently—not as the stoic warrior or the enigmatic leader, but as someone who, for the first time, looked...unsure.

"I had no idea," he said quietly. "That...that changes things."

Dante, ever the mediator, stepped in. "It doesn't matter where she came from," he said firmly. "What matters is who she is now and what she's capable of. And right now, she's one of us."

Reed's eyes flickered with a doubt he quickly buried beneath resolve. "Absolutely," he stated firmly. "We're all here to help. Amnesia explains some things, but it also raises more questions. If you don't remember your past, figuring out your abilities might be even more complicated."

Giles nodded, a knowing look in his eyes. "Indeed, the past can be elusive," he said carefully, his tone measured, as if weighing his words.

"But that doesn't mean it's lost forever. We'll find a way to uncover it together, Lenox. You've already made it this far on your own—and as Dante said, now you have us to help."

He paused, his gaze steady. "And remember, the past has a way of catching up with us, whether we remember it or not."

I managed a small smile, relief mingled with lingering uncertainty settling in my chest. It was comforting to know they didn't see me as a freak, but opening up about my past—or lack thereof—had left me feeling exposed, like a nerve laid bare.

For a moment, it felt like I was standing on a precipice, exposed to the elements. But beneath the uncertainty, a flicker of determination sparked. I wasn't just a victim of circumstance. The pieces of my life may have been scattered, but

I'd find a way to put them back together. And if that meant facing more shadows, so be it.

"Thanks." I directed a watery smile at all of them. "I appreciate that. More than you know." Despite the unshed tears clogging my throat, I forced a cheerful tone. "So...what now?"

Reed's gaze was steady, his earlier intensity replaced with something softer, almost protective. "Now, we train," he said. "We help you understand your powers and control them."

Giles clapped his hands, breaking the tension. "Good. Now that that's settled, I've got some fresh scones in the kitchen. Why don't we take a break before we dive into anything else?"

A collective sigh of relief went up around the room. We filed out of the study, moving toward the warm, inviting kitchen. The smell of freshly baked goods was a welcome change from the intensity of the discussion.

As we gathered around the kitchen island, nibbling on Giles's scones, Derek nudged me with his elbow. "So," he said quietly, his tone shifting to a more serious note. "My parents are pushing to find Emily's...well, to give her a proper burial."

He cleared his throat. "I, uh, was planning to head over there tomorrow, if you, um, are still up for helping?"

I nodded, swallowing a bite of my scone. "Absolutely. We need to get some answers, and I want to help you get closure."

Derek gave a grateful smile, his eyes softening. "Thanks, Lenox. It means a lot." He paused, glancing around the room to ensure the others were engrossed in their own conversations. "And about the amnesia and this training... You going to be okay?"

I shrugged, trying to keep my voice light. "I'll manage. At least I won't be doing it alone."

Derek chuckled softly. "Yeah, well, I've got your back, you know that."

I smiled, a warm feeling settling in my chest. "I know, Derek. I appreciate it."

The moment of camaraderie hung between us, a small comfort amid the chaos. The warmth of the tea seeped into my hands, grounding me in the present. Around me, the soft murmur of voices blended with the clink of china, creating a fragile sense of normalcy.

But beneath it all, the weight of what lay ahead pressed on my chest, both daunting and exhilarating. The future would bring new challenges—new opportunities to learn about my past and my powers.

However, before that, I'd have to face the ghosts of someone else's past. Who knew what secrets Emily's spirit might reveal—or what dangers it might attract?

25

LOST AND FOUND

Derek's childhood home in Black Creek, a quiet community west of Savannah, exuded comfort and affluence with its wide front porch and sprawling grounds. As we approached, I caught a glimpse of a meandering creek running along the back of the property. Towering oaks and scruffy pines dotted the area, and I wondered which had been Emily's tree.

Derek's parents met us at the door, their faces a blend of hope and trepidation. As we crossed the porch, a taller, older version of Derek, extended his hand, his grip firm yet warm.

"Hello, I'm Paul. Janet and I...we're grateful for everything you've done so far." He glanced at the petite woman at his side, his gaze softening as he looked at her. "And we really appreciate you coming here today, agreeing to help us again."

Tension radiated from both of them—fear and anticipation mingling in the space between us. It was clear they were desperate for answers, clinging to the hope that today might bring them some measure of peace.

Janet nodded, her eyes misty. "Yes, thank you. It means more than you know. We just want to bring Emily home."

A sharp pang of sorrow pierced my heart. This family had been through so much, and I only hoped I could help them find some peace.

I offered a soft smile. "I'm sorry we're meeting under these circumstances," I began, sensing the weight of their hopes. "I'll do my best, but I have to be honest—it's important to manage expectations."

The eagerness in Janet's eyes cut me to the quick. "Sometimes spirits aren't clear, or they don't fully understand what happened to them or where they are. I just...I don't want to promise something I can't deliver."

Janet swallowed hard, her voice trembling. "I understand. It's just...she's our little girl. We have to try." Her voice broke on a sob, and tears sprang to her eyes. She swiped at them with the back of her hand and gave a ragged laugh.

"Oh, where are my manners?" She sniffed and held the door open. "Come in, come in and make yourself comfortable. Can I get you anything? I made a pot of tea."

"Tea would be lovely." I smiled and followed her inside. Derek guided me to the sunroom, past family photos lining the hallway—memories of happier times that seemed to whisper from the walls.

Derek and his father were talking quietly, so I took the time to examine the sunroom while we waited for Janet to join us. The room was filled with light, the glass walls offering a panoramic view of the backyard that stretched to meet the dense line of trees at the creek's edge. The ceiling fans spun lazily overhead, casting soft shadows across the floor.

It was a tranquil space, the kind where one could easily lose track of time watching the water flow. Today, though, that peace was tinged with a sense of urgency.

Janet returned with a tray of tea, her hands trembling slightly as she set it down. "Here we are," she said, forcing a smile. "I hope you like Earl Grey."

"Thank you, it's fine," I replied softly, taking a cup and letting the warmth seep into my hands. Derek's eyes flicked to mine, a silent question hanging between us.

I nodded slightly, indicating I was ready to begin. The room fell into a hushed stillness, everyone holding their breath, waiting for whatever might come next.

I closed my eyes, taking a deep breath, and focused on the image of Emily as I'd seen her in the police station. "Emily," I called softly in my mind, my voice steady yet gentle.

"Emily, if you can hear me, I'm here with your family. They want to talk to you...they miss you."

I repeated my call several times and then paused as I sensed a change in the room. The air seemed to thicken like fog on a rainy morning.

A familiar prickle ran up my spine as if someone were watching me from a distance. And then I felt it—a light, almost playful tug at the corner of my consciousness, like a child tugging at a sleeve.

I opened my eyes, and there she was, standing by the window. She looked just as I remembered her: a little girl with cornflower blue eyes and a bright, infectious smile.

"Hi, Lenox!" she chirped, her voice clear and cheerful, as if she were greeting a friend in the park.

Despite the somberness of the occasion, I couldn't help but grin. She was such a sweet child, taken far too soon. I glanced at the sofa to see Janet and Paul perched on the edge, their eyes darting between me and the empty space where Emily stood.

I could feel their tension, their desperate hope that today might bring them closer to their daughter, even if they couldn't see or hear her themselves.

"Is she…is she here?" Janet asked, her voice barely above a whisper, her eyes misting with unshed tears.

I nodded, keeping my gaze on Emily. "She's here," I said softly. "Emily, your mommy and daddy and Derek are here. They want to talk to you."

Emily's eyes brightened. "Hi, Mama! Hi, Daddy! Hi Derek!" Her voice was filled with joy as she waved energetically.

"They can't see you, sweetheart," I explained gently. "But they can hear what you want to tell them through me."

Janet's hand flew to her mouth, and Paul leaned forward, his knuckles white as he gripped the armrests of his chair.

"Can she... can she hear us?" Paul asked, his voice tight with emotion.

"Yes," I assured him, glancing briefly at the parents before returning my focus to Emily. "She can hear you."

Paul cleared his throat, struggling to keep his composure. "Emily...sweetheart," he began, his voice shaking. "Are you...are you okay?"

Emily grinned and nodded eagerly. "I'm okay, Daddy," she said, her words flowing through me as if they were my own. "I've been playing with Scout!"

A tear slid down Janet's cheek. She whispered that Scout was the family dog as she wiped it away with a trembling hand. "Oh, Emily...we miss you so much," she whispered, her voice breaking.

"I miss you too, Mama," Emily replied, a hint of childlike innocence in her tone.

I relayed the message, and Janet let out a soft, tearful laugh, blending sorrow and relief.

Derek shifted in his seat, his face set in a serious expression. "Emily," he said softly, his tone both gentle and urgent, "do you remember what happened to you, where you were the last time... the last time we saw you?"

Emily's bright expression faltered, and a look of guilt came over her small face. She cast her head down and traced a pattern with her tennis shoe. "I'm sorry," she murmured, then looked up at me with wide, sorrowful eyes.

"Tell them, Lenox, please! I didn't...I broke the rules...I'm so sorry, Mama!"

My breath caught at the desperation and sorrow in her eyes. My hands shook as I turned to Janet and Paul, trying to maintain control of my emotions. "She says she's sorry," I relayed, my voice breaking. "She broke the rules...she didn't mean to..."

Janet's breath hitched, and she leaned forward, tears spilling down her cheeks. "Oh, sweetheart," she whispered, her voice thick with emotion. "It's okay, baby. We forgive you. You didn't do anything wrong."

I turned back to Emily, who was now nervously twisting the hem of her t-shirt. "Emily," I said gently, "can you tell me where you were? What rules did you break?"

Emily looked confused, her small face scrunching up as if trying to remember. "Don't talk to strangers," she began, her voice wavering between fear and childlike repetition. "Stay in the yard. Look both ways. Brush your teeth. You're too little. Don't climb. It's not ready. Put your clothes in the hamper. Don't talk to strangers. Stay in the..." She began to repeat herself, the same phrases looping in her soft, almost melodic tone.

I held up a hand, gently interrupting. "Emily, wait a second." Her voice faded to a whisper, and I turned back to Derek and his parents. "She keeps repeating a list of rules...things like 'stay in the yard, brush your teeth, you're too little, and um ,don't climb, put your clothes in the hamper, it's not ready.' Does any of that mean something to you?"

Janet let out a watery laugh, the sound trembling with both sorrow and a bittersweet fondness. "Oh, my baby girl," she murmured, her voice thick with emotion. "Always getting into things. So curious, so full of life."

She chuckled softly, wiping away a tear. "I'm not surprised she remembers the 'no climbing' rule. She was such a little monkey! I was forever telling her to stay out of the trees, that she wasn't Tarzan. And don't even get me started on her Spider-Man phase!"

She glanced at Derek, a sad smile on her lips. "Once you took her to see that movie, it's all she talked about! She even took nails from the garage and drove them into her wall so she could practice her 'Spidey senses.' Do you remember, Paul?"

Paul sniffed, a faint smile touching his lips as he nodded. "Do I," he said, his voice a low rumble filled with both love and heartache. "Spent a whole weekend patching those holes and repainting. She always kept us on our toes."

Derek, who had been listening intently, suddenly sat up straighter. "Hold on," he interjected, his gaze darting between me and his mother. "Lenox, what did Emily say after 'don't climb'?"

I closed my eyes briefly, recalling Emily's words. "She said, 'it's not ready.' Why? Does that mean something to you?"

Derek's eyes widened, realization dawning on his face. He shot up from his chair. "Yes," he said, almost breathless. "I know where she went. The rec center playground. It was under construction at the time and they were installing a climbing wall, and she was obsessed with it. She kept asking when she could try it out, but we always said it wasn't ready yet."

Janet's breath hitched, and she covered her mouth with her hand, eyes widening. "Oh my God," she whispered. "The climbing wall. She wouldn't stop talking about it."

Paul looked at Derek, his expression caught between skepticism and hope. "Do you think that's where she went?"

Derek nodded, determination lighting up his eyes. "It has to be. She always wanted to be Spider-Man. It makes sense now."

I stood, a shiver racing through me. "Then we need to go there. Now."

The rec center playground was quiet, the usual sounds of playing children absent. It was eerie, standing in front of the bright, cheerful equipment that now seemed out of place against the backdrop of what we were about to uncover.

Two officers met us at the entrance. Derek had called them on the way. They were friends of the family and greeted us with a somber professionalism.

"We appreciate you both coming out," Derek said, shaking their hands firmly. "We have a lead on where Emily might be...where she was...last."

One of the officers, a broad-shouldered man with a weathered face, nodded. "We'll do whatever we can to help, Derek. Just point us in the right direction."

Derek glanced at me, a silent question in his eyes. I nodded, then took a step back from the group, pretending to scan the area. My heart pounded in my chest as I tried to keep my actions subtle, my voice low. I closed my eyes and took a deep breath, focusing inward once again.

"Emily," I called out in my mind, my voice steady yet soft. "Emily, can you show us where you were?"

The air grew colder almost immediately, a chill settling over my skin. I opened my eyes to see Emily standing a few feet in front of a door marked "Mechanical Room." Her small frame shook, her eyes wide with fear, locked on the door, whispering to herself.

I moved closer to Derek, keeping my voice just above a whisper, careful not to draw too much attention from the officers. "She's here," I murmured, glancing at Derek. "She's looking at that door. The mechanical room."

Derek nodded and, motioning for the officers to follow, stepped into the room. The dim overhead light revealed a cluttered space filled with pipes, electrical panels, machinery.

Emily remained at the threshold, her eyes wide, her body trembling. She was whispering again, her voice a low, urgent murmur. "Hate surprises...want to climb, hate it...hate the dark..."

I took a deep breath, trying to keep my voice steady. "Emily, what is it? Can you show me where you were?" I asked, still trying to maintain a low profile. But as her fear escalated, I found it harder to keep my composure.

The officers began to search, moving boxes and crates, peering behind stacks of equipment. Derek followed, his eyes scanning every corner as he moved slowly, methodically.

"This is stupid," Derek muttered after a few moments. "None of this would have been here back then. We need to think about what was here when she disappeared."

He walked over to the HVAC unit, crouching down to inspect it. The officers joined him, their lights illuminating the metal casing and the tangle of pipes and wires. "It's just the furnace," one of them said, sounding uncertain. "Nothing here from that time."

"No," Derek said. "This was a remodel and addition. The furnace would have already been here."

Emily's whispering grew louder, her words tumbling over each other in a frantic stream. "Dark...no...don't put me in...dark...hate surprises..."

The intensity of her fear washed over me like a wave, and I instinctively clamped my hands over my ears as her whispers grew into a shriek. A tremor ran through my body, my breath quickening as I tried to maintain control.

"Derek, she's upset...really upset now that you're over there," I managed to say through gritted teeth, my caution forgotten in the face of Emily's mounting terror.

Beside me, Janet was trembling, tears streaming down her face. She clung to Paul, her eyes wide with fear. "What is she saying?" she asked, her voice barely a whisper, filled with a mother's desperation.

I hesitated, torn between sparing them the details and knowing they deserved the truth. "She...she doesn't want to be put somewhere and, um, hates the dark," I relayed, my voice breaking. A wave of nausea hit me at the raw terror in Emily's voice, wishing I could shield them all from the horror.

Janet raised a trembling hand to her mouth and sobbed.

Derek paled, his jaw tightening as he processed my words. "This area was incomplete at the time. You could see inside because they hadn't completed all of the walls. It was mostly rough framing, covered in dust because they were hanging the drywall..." He turned to me again. "Lenox, Emily said dark, right?"

I nodded, my hands still pressing against my ears, trying to block out the piercing sound of Emily's shrieks. "Yes, she keeps saying 'dark...don't put me in...don't...dark...'"

Derek straightened, his eyes narrowing as he scanned the room. His gaze locked onto the walls near the HVAC unit. "We need to look inside the walls," he said, his voice steely with resolve.

One of the officers shook his head. "We can't just tear into the walls, Derek. We need permission—"

"Permission?" Paul's voice cut through the room, sharp with anger and grief. He strode over to a toolbox near the doorway and pulled out a hammer, his body trembling with rage. "She's my daughter. I don't need permission."

Before anyone could stop him, Paul swung the hammer at the wall, aiming wildly at the section near the furnace. Bits of plaster flew, cascading around him as he continued to hammer, driven by a father's desperate rage and grief. His blows were relentless, each swing more forceful than the last, his pain echoing with every impact.

The officers tried to intervene, but Paul was beyond reason, lost in the need to find his daughter. He struck again, the hammer biting deep into the wall, and with a particularly vicious swing, an entire section gave way, crumbling to the floor in a cloud of dust.

Derek moved quickly, stepping forward to peer into the exposed cavity. His breath caught in his throat as he saw the dark, narrow space between the studs. "Oh God," he whispered, his voice barely audible. "Dad...Dad, stop."

But Paul swung again, his hammer crashing through the remaining drywall. The officers rushed forward, trying to pull him back, but he shrugged them off, his eyes wild with grief.

"Dad!" Derek shouted, grabbing his father's arm. "Stop! We found her." His voice broke on a sob. "We found Emily."

Paul's hammer slipped from his grasp, clattering to the floor as he fell to his knees. Janet stumbled over to him, collapsing beside him. They wrapped their arms around each other, their bodies trembling with the weight of their grief, their cries filling the room with a raw, heartbreaking sound.

Emily's shrieking stopped, and I looked up to see her standing at the entrance, her small body trembling, tears streaming down her face. "Hate surprises," she whispered one last time, her voice filled with a quiet, haunting sadness.

Derek crouched against the wall, his head bowed, silent tears streaming down his face. He looked lost, as if the discovery had shattered something inside him. His hand pressed against the cold wall that had been his sister's tomb, his shoulders shaking with quiet sobs.

I knelt beside Paul and Janet first, my hand resting on Paul's shoulder as I murmured softly, "She's at peace now. She's free." I stayed with them for a moment, feeling their grief like a physical weight, then I rose and walked over to Derek.

He hadn't moved, still crouched against the wall, his body racked with silent sobs. Without a word, I wrapped my arms around him, pulling him close. He tensed for a moment, and then his arms came around me, holding on as if he were afraid to let go.

I didn't speak; there were no words that could heal the wound that had just been ripped open. I just held him, offering what little comfort I could as he grieved for the sister he had finally found and lost all over again.

As the officers began to clear the room, one of them radioed for the coroner. The world outside felt impossibly distant, a million miles away from this small, dark room where a family's worst fears had just been confirmed.

But I knew, deep down, that we had done what we came here to do. Emily had been found. And maybe now, finally, this family could start to heal.

26

SHADOWS
RISING

A warm breeze whispered through the live oaks dot-
ting the landscape of Colonial Park Cemetery, setting the Spanish moss swaying like tendrils of mist. Killing
time before my next tour group arrived, I wandered closer
to the wrought iron gates and peered through the bars.

The evening light played tricks, shifting and stretching
the fleeting shadows that danced over the graves and stat-
ues. My gaze landed on a marble angel, its wings partially
cloaked in moss, face bowed in prayer. It reminded me of
Emily's funeral—how she had stood beside me, watching
it unfold.

I had been surprised her spirit hadn't found peace yet.
Though I hadn't asked her why, part of me suspected it
had something to do with the justice she was still owed.

After helping Amelia and Emily, I no longer questioned whether my abilities were a curse. These last few months had shown me that, though the darkness could be terrifying, there would always be light to counter it.

But there was something else—a quiet uncertainty that gnawed at the edges of my thoughts. I could open portals, communicate with the dead, share my energy...but was that the limit of my abilities? Or was there more?

The thought unsettled me. If I could do this much, what else might I be capable of? And could I control it?

As these questions about my gifts lingered, so did the memories I had yet to recover. But I didn't fear the future as I once had. Not with Giles, Derek, and the others by my side. I knew now that I wasn't alone.

Still, as I considered the powers I already had, I couldn't help but wonder—was I truly ready for whatever came next?

A rasping groan echoed through the stillness, sending goosebumps racing up my arms despite the heat of the evening. Heart pounding, I spun around, scanning the deserted street while telling myself it was just the wind or maybe a stray cat prowling in the shadows.

Seeing nothing out of the ordinary, I let out a shaky breath and rolled my eyes. Giles's concerns about the recent spate of missing people had clearly gotten to me.

Feeling foolish, I turned back toward the park when something caught my eye. A long, narrow shape, dark and indistinct, moved along the fence line at the back of the grounds.

Frowning, I stepped closer to the gate, squinting through the bars. Another low, guttural growl rumbled from the depths of the park, echoing off the tombs. My eyes widened, and a lump rose in my throat. That...that was not a cat.

The odd shape shifted again, wisps of black smoke curling through the fog drifting up from the river. I tried to rationalize it—maybe someone had a fire pit nearby, or perhaps it was just the trick of the dim light—but the way it moved, too deliberate, too fluid, set my nerves on edge. Then it turned.

Glowing red eyes locked with mine, piercing through the dark. My heart slammed against my chest as Maris's warning echoed in my mind.

The necromancer was gone, but something darker was rising.

THE HUNT BEGINS...

Did you notice the hidden clues in Shadow Gifts?

Seven hidden ghosts are on the Savannah map at the front of

the book.

PLUS, one chapter contains a secret icon—the first piece of

a puzzle that spans the series.

Collect the clues, solve the puzzle, and unlock a hidden trea-

sure!

Then...

If you loved the adventure,

leave a review to let other readers know what they're miss-

ing,

and don't forget to pre-order Shadow Betrayal today to con-

tinue the journey into the shadows.

Happy hunting!

The Shadow Destiny Series

(Urban Fantasy Mystery)

Shadow Gifts

Shadow Betrayal (Pre-Order)

The Holly Daye Mystery Series

Hounds and Heists

(free prequel)

Masquerades and Murder

Carolers and Corpses

Priests and Poison

Plantations and Allegations

Scarecrows and Scandals

<u>The Cosmic Café Mystery Series</u>

Fey Goes to Jail

(Free Prequel)

Ring of Lies

Holly Jolly Jabbed

Broken Chords

Hey there, thanks for finishing my book! You already know I'm a writer *(obviously, since you made it to the end)*, but I'm also a mom, a grandma, an animal lover, and a longtime Lowcountry local who's deeply inspired by the history and mystery of the South.

My journey into writing is just as winding and unpredictable as a haunted Savannah street. Back in 2011, I published my first book, Ring of Lies, but life had a few surprises up its sleeve.

Between homeschooling, helping my husband start a business, and later managing a grocery store department *(where my best story ideas often came while stocking shelves!)*, my passion for storytelling never disappeared. I even carried a sharpie in my pocket to scribble plot ideas on cardboard boxes!

In the end, it was the call of creativity that won out. Now, I write full time, blending my love for the eerie charm of the South with a fascination for ghost stories, mysteries, and magic. My latest series, *Shadow Destiny*, takes you into Savannah's haunted streets, where ghosts have stories to tell, secrets are buried deep, and not everything is as it seems.

Want to stay connected? Join my newsletter, Coastal Shadows, where I dive into everything from writing updates to behind-the-scenes looks at the Lowcountry's spookiest spots. You'll even get a peek into my life—complete with a menagerie of animals and occasional day trips to the most beautiful (*and haunted!*) places in the South.

You can sign up at www.rachellynneauthor.com and find me on Instagram and Facebook for more updates, recipes, fun reads, and general chaos!

I can't wait to share more stories with you—see you in the shadows!

Rachel

Shadow Betrayal

Book 2 in the Shadow Destiny Series

Demanding ghosts, moody fae, and disappearing locals are an average day for Lenox Grady—eh, normal is over-rated, anyway ...

Lenox Grady's life is finally starting to settle into something almost normal—if your definition of normal includes being an errand girl for ghosts and keeping an enigmatic fae happy while mastering the delicate art of avoiding the accidental destruction of multiple realms!

But just as Lenox finds her footing in this strange new reality, the peaceful façade of Savannah begins to crack, and something sinister stirs in the shadows.

When locals start vanishing without a trace, whispers of dark magic once again rise, putting Lenox in the crosshairs, and trusting the wrong person leaves Lenox fighting a force determined to erase her from the world she's only just begun to call her own.

Ready to dive back into the shadows with Lenox? Don't miss the next thrilling installment in the Shadow Destiny series. Secure your copy now and be among the first to unravel the mysteries lurking in the dark.

Pre-order Shadow Betrayal today!

Made in the USA
Middletown, DE
01 May 2025

75004844R00203